OUTBACK TREASURE

Noelene Jenkinson

Chapter 1

As Darcy Manning travelled west on her second long challenging day out from Brisbane, she eyed off the outback Queensland scenery and drew the same conclusion as anyone might out here – that the country was dry, flat and isolated.

Despite her padded leather seat, extended stretches at a time on her cruiser motorbike was a nightmare on the backside so every few hours she peeled off the tarmac onto the roadside and took a break. The clear blue winter sky only magnified the outback's vast open spaces. She had never explored this country before, in some aspects so different to the tropical heat and desert roads of the Northern Territory where she had been raised, yet it was so similar in its endless horizon.

An outback woman down to her favourite etched leather boots, to another's eyes this remote landscape might look like nothing and seem like it held even less. But after working in the city, Darcy had leapt at the chance when it was offered to escape out here again even though it was only for two weeks because she loved her work with a passion.

Ditching the freeways and racing lanes of traffic, despite Brisbane being nestled along the curves of its pretty winding river setting, was the craziest sense of freedom. Darcy wanted to let out a typical tomboy whoop of joy to be returning to anywhere outback. If it was away from a city, she loved it all.

Running her appreciative excited gaze over the Mitchell grass plains, there was no denying this was tough country. Only the clumps of deep rooted scattered tussocks could survive the droughts out here and tolerate the harsh environment.

As she rode, Darcy's attention strayed further away from the straight isolated road toward the distant mesa escarpment known as jump-up, abrupt rises out of the plains.

Today its red earth, ochre colours and seasonal green after the summer monsoon rains gave no hint of its origins millions of years before. This, her palaeontologist heart swelled, was dinosaur country. Once an ancient inland sea. A rich watery wonderland filled with marine life. Who would guess that herds of massive creatures once roamed this land?

Darcy knew the culture, beliefs and rituals of the local Aboriginal people also stretched back to distant times, post dinosaurs. Their own story, too, evolved over tens of thousands of years and was the world's longest continuous culture. Its history carved into rock faces, continuing today with stories, dancing and art.

Caring for country, the traditional land to which an indigenous person belonged, was the responsibility taken on by their communities.

They believed in a time known as The Dreaming that explained creation and the nature of the world, the place of every person in it and the importance of tradition. The Dreaming described their ancestral domain, teaching people about country and where food, water and shelter was found.

Darcy always made sure there was an indigenous member on every dig for there was always much they knew that was of advantage to her team.

Despite the isolation, Darcy had never been able to pinpoint the words to describe the greatness that was country life. She just knew it as a feeling sitting deep and powerful in her heart, and singing in the blood that flowed through her veins.

And this particular landscape drew her even more because of the treasures it held just below the topsoil. Okay, sometimes it took a little digging deeper. But scratching in dirt for that next fossil find was in her top three of life's pleasures along with having sex – not that she had experienced that one in a while - and an ice cold beer on a stinking hot day.

Her purpose this visit was on a mission for the Museum to identify and assess a new fossil discovery on an outback sheep station, *Matilda Downs*. Then to manage and supervise the volunteer field team along with the supply trailer of digging equipment already organised to come out in convoy to the dig site tomorrow. With all legalities and the holder permit organised, the search could begin straight away. Always an exciting time.

Apparently the station owner's son had been out mustering sheep and, being an outback boy who knew every rock on the station, figured some looked different, brought them back to the homestead, took photos and emailed them off to the Museum. Which is where she came in.

In recent years the institution had named three new Australian dinosaurs, the first for 75 years. With its rich dinosaur heritage, Queensland boasted the most comprehensive fossil history in Australia. The Museum's collection alone numbered millions of species including the country's oldest dinosaur skeleton.

From the images the boy had sent, it was difficult to accurately identify the find but initial guesses centred on it being a potentially significant section of dinosaur skeleton. Every new discovery was great news for Australian paleontology because each one provided more information on where it sat on the growing sauropod family tree and its geographic context.

Less than an hour later, bum sore and weary, Darcy pulled over onto the roadside to exercise her long jeans-clad legs, shake her long dark hair free from the helmet to cool her neck while she swigged from the water bottle in her pack. *Damn, what's not to love about a country view?* she muttered, eyes narrowed to a squint despite sunglasses against the day's high glare.

She breathed deep a few times, did a 360 and swiped water from her mouth with the back of her hand. Recapping the lid, she stowed the bottle, clipped on her helmet then fired her bike into life and took it easy for the run into Winton.

She had pitched her tent in Carnarvon Gorge last night in a picturesque semi-secluded camp under a canopy of gums. After a refreshing night's sleep, she had woken to sunlight streaming over the tops of the white sandstone cliffs towering above the steep gorge. Lunch in Longreach seemed forever ago so she was hanging out for a late arvo beer in a pub. Fortunately Winton had four of them.

She would leave it for another day to visit the huge Australian Age of Dinosaur museum complex half an hour south east of town to drool over the largest collection of Australian dinosaur bones in the world. Darcy had already been in touch and liaised to organise the field team but, for now, she only planned on stopping long enough in Winton for a cold one because she wanted to make the station and pitch camp by dark.

After a few years of working mainly in museums and only occasionally daring to venture back onto any new winter dig site, wary to participate and leave herself open to judgement again, feeling the uncomfortable need to look over her shoulder, Darcy decided this time to accept responsibility for the *Matilda Downs* dig when it was offered and plough ahead, embracing the opportunity and new discoveries. Always a high.

She released a long sigh of pleasure. It was great to be in the outback again.

As she cruised into Winton, Darcy's professional mind darted over the fact of the first discovery of a fossilised dinosaur footprint on a station property in the 1960s in this region. The small country town was also the birthplace of the iconic Australian folk song *Waltzing Matilda* and the now international airline Qantas.

But in more recent decades, the area was becoming known for the explosion of much older ancient dinosaur fossil finds that had begun a tourist stampede.

She slowed at a corner two storey pub, turned her bike around and backed it into the kerb alongside dusty four wheel drives and utes. Inside, she settled on a seat at the bar with its rows of glasses suspended above from massive logs of wood. Individual rustic touch, Darcy thought. She ordered a schooner.

As he handed her the icy cold frothy beer, the barman smiled and asked pleasantly, 'Where you headed?'

'*Matilda Downs.*'

'Beaumont territory. Need directions?'

Darcy shook her head and tapped her sat phone. 'GPS. Thanks all the same.' Because she had grown up among them, the friendliness and hospitality of country people never surprised her.

'How far have you come?'

'Brissie.'

'City girl, huh?'

'Nope. Territory girl originally.'

He moved down the bar to serve two new customers. Grey nomads by the look of it. Retired travellers who all trailed north to warmer climes when winter closed in down south.

Unaware of admiring male glances from fellow drinkers in the pub, Darcy sipped her beer as she checked her mobile for any messages. With no phone service anywhere remote, Darcy had a sat sleeve on hers and flipped the switch to activate it. She made short work of her bubbly amber drink while texting her location and an update response to the Museum. Using her phone map, she made tracks for *Matilda Downs,* sending a wave and cheerful goodbye to the barman as she left.

She clipped on her helmet, legged it over the bike, revved the cruiser into life and continued heading west for the last part of her two-day trek. She could have flown to Longreach then grabbed a regional flight on to Winton but where would have been the fun in that? Darcy reflected on all the countryside and scenery she would have missed flying over it at twenty thousand feet.

Keeping an eye out for the turn off from the sealed highway, a half hour later the station property sign easily caught her gaze. She slowed and turned left, hitting her first stretch of dirt since motoring into the gorge the night before, hundreds of kilometres back.

She took it steady, following the bumpy gravelled road in for a few miles before signs of life appeared ahead, the late afternoon sun already lowering off to her right. The outback was famous for magnificent sunsets so she looked forward to admiring many while she was out here.

She had read the stats on *Matilda Downs* station. Hundreds of thousands of acres apparently, and sheep, with the property in the Beaumont family for generations.

When an oasis of trees suddenly rose from the flat plains and a sprawling timber Queenslander loomed into sight, growing larger as she approached, raised off the ground on low stumps with typical verandas all around, a glinting tin roof and chimneys, Darcy knew she had arrived.

Darcy's warm gaze spread over the big old square homestead. It looked like most rooms had French windows that opened out directly onto the broad wrap-around veranda. A common extension of living space out here, revealed by lots of cane and timber seating with random cushions and small tables.

She hoped the dig site wasn't too much further on. She was bushed but on a property this size it could still be some distance away. Two dogs raced out to greet her.

She drew to a stop in a cloud of dust, alighted from the bike and pulled off her helmet to shake out her long dark hair. Finally freed from being mostly covered for two days, Darcy let the slightest hint of late afternoon breeze flick its ends and cool her down.

Distracted by the two beautiful working collie dogs, Darcy bent to give them attention. They panted and lapped it up before she straightened and whipped her gaze toward the sound of a door slamming and booted feet slowly descending the front steps with familiar ease.

Holy cow. Darcy's interest sprang to alert as the man's wavy sandy hair, bleached from a life outdoors, disappeared beneath a broad well-worn Akubra when big hands set it on his head. Powerful legs in dusty Wranglers and a chest tight in a checked shirt, strode forward to meet her, bringing his rugged body closer.

In their phone conversation when Nina Beaumont had said her son made a fossil find, Darcy imagined a kid. This strapping cowboy was too young to be Nina's husband. Could this fully grown handsome outback man be the *boy* of their conversation? How wrong could you be?

Either way, the vision splendid was nothing new. She had encountered more than her share of brown and muscled outback men in her time. Damn, she'd been in the city too long and forgotten how sexy country boys could be.

Somehow she managed to remember how to breathe and whipped on a casual smile to speak first. 'Darcy Manning.'

'Mitch Beaumont.'

He extended a hand and captured a smaller softer one in his. There were plenty of tropical storms out here in summer during the Wet but he'd never been struck by lightning until today.

A country honey on a motor bike was their Doctor palaeontologist? Next few weeks looked promising.

He tried not to stare and laugh at her tee shirt as she removed her leather jacket and gloves to sling them over the bike. For one, she would think him a pervert eyeing off the breasts pushing it out when in reality the slogan emblazoned across the front was a hoot. *I'm a palaeontologist. Nothing scares me.* Based on first impressions, he believed her manner reflected a strong personality. But the damage was done. She'd tracked his gaze.

'You can read,' she quipped wryly, catching his stifled grin.

He liked her sense of humour. Some girls got huffy. He nodded to the slogan. 'Is that true?'

She planted her hands on slim hips and squinted at him. 'Pretty much. You the fossil hunter?'

He nodded. 'All my life. Come inside. Mother has smoko for you in the kitchen.'

'Great. I only grabbed a quick beer in the pub and I'm thirsty again already.'

'I'm sure another could be arranged.'

'Tea will be just fine.'

He stepped aside allowing her to pass, inhaling a whiff of something feminine but musky. The view of a neat backside in jeans swaying as she climbed the steps ahead of him didn't go unappreciated either.

Both automatically tugged off their boots on the veranda. Mitch reached around her to open the door, accidentally pressing close during the gesture. She tossed him a sharp brown-eyed gaze of surprise. He thought it was offence from the contact but when she whispered *Thanks* he was relieved and tossed his hat onto its usual outside chair near the door.

Darcy felt a rush of cool air as she stepped inside the homestead at one end of a long wide central hallway dividing the house. With the strategic opening of doors and windows, certainly necessary during summer's stifling tropical heat, but even on mildly warm winter days like today, clever refreshing breezes streamed through.

As Mitch led and she followed, they passed open doors either side, drawing Darcy's attention to teasing glimpses of comfortable old furniture and polished timber floors, although they walked on a soft well-worn carpet runner down the hall. A gallery of family photographs, black and whites, sepia and later ones in colour, lined both walls all the way down.

All senses couldn't help but be drawn to the aromas of baking just before entering a vast open country kitchen with a double range and lots of cream timber panelled cupboards. A big central wooden table was set with a smoko feast, one plate draped with a tea towel, probably keeping fresh scones warm, a thickly sliced fruit cake on a bread board and yet another plate of crunchy looking biscuits.

Above the sink to one side a huge window spread views across a stretch of mowed grass surrounded by a hardy tended garden to homestead yards and gum trees with jump up mesas beyond. A trim short woman with curly grey hair clad in fitted jeans and a pale blue checked shirt with her back to them as they entered, turned at their arrival and beamed from washing dishes in the sink. So, the son had inherited his blue eyes from his mother.

She dried her hands and stepped forward. 'I'm Nina and you will be Doctor Manning,' she said in a decisive soft voice.

Up close her tanned complexion was no longer smooth and lines spread out from the corners of observant sparkling eyes. The firm hand shake in greeting revealed a strong personality, in contrast with her petite but wiry stature. Darcy guessed a fellow countrywoman born and bred, too.

'Darcy. A lovely old place you have here.'

'It's been home to the Beaumonts for three generations. Gets a face lift now and then. Would you like to freshen up, dear?'

'Appreciate it.'

If only to check her appearance as well as pee. She hadn't looked at him directly since entering the kitchen but she could feel sexy Beaumont's blue eyes all over her. A compliment maybe on the scarcity of women in the outback but wherever they did live, they worked hard alongside their men, created a home often out of difficult conditions and supported them one hundred per cent. She would be willing to bet Nina Beaumont had been doing just that all her life alongside her own husband.

Braving a glance in the bathroom mirror, Darcy groaned. God she looked a mess. She dampened her long dark hair in places and combed fingers through to free the knots. She usually pulled it back in a ponytail or at her nape with a tie but it was too bulky under her bike helmet so, for the last two days, she left it all down.

She foamed up the hand wash, dabbing some over her face and neck because it smelled so nice and, right now, her appearance could do with a lift. When the dig crew and supply trailers came out tomorrow, she looked forward to the solar camp shower. But for now she shrugged. She'd have to do.

As she crossed the hall again, Darcy heard dogs barking and boots clomp up the front steps and onto the veranda.

'That'll be Ed,' Nina explained as she re-entered the kitchen, setting a teapot on a table mat.

Mitch lounged against a kitchen bench opposite and sent her a lazy disturbing glance. Darcy didn't have time to dwell on her body's wilful reaction because the new arrival bowled into the room, dusty, suntanned, thinning hair and smiling. An older version of his son. An open honest man Darcy instantly liked. From personal experience, she had always found outback folk down-to-earth genuine.

'That your motor bike young lady?' he asked her in a strong gravelly voice, a twitch of a grin edging his mouth.

'Yes, sir.' Darcy restrained her amusement.

'Nice looking machine. I'm Ed. Guess you're Doctor Manning.' He thrust out a sun browned arm.

'Darcy,' she and Nina said together.

The two women locked gazes and laughed while Darcy's hand was gripped in a firm handshake.

'Well then Darcy, welcome to *Matilda Downs*.'

'Sit down and help yourself everyone,' Nina said. 'How do you take your tea, Darcy?'

'Black straight up.'

Nina poured a mug from the teapot and handed it across the table. Ed pulled out a chair at the end and, without ceremony, grabbed a slice of cake before he sat down. With an unhurried deliberation, Mitch moved away from the bench and pulled out a chair opposite, accepting the mug of white tea his mother served and adding two heaped spoons of sugar. So, he liked things sweet, huh. She wondered if that preference extended to women. Might mean they weren't destined to get along.

Irritatingly, her interest deepened and she found his focus troubling because he was staring directly at her and saying nothing. A powerful and telling silence.

Darcy briefly cut the connection while she looked away and helped herself to a scone, breaking it open and lacing it with butter. But she knew that sooner or later she must address the reason for this visit which meant she'd have to open up a conversation with him. Might as well do it sooner rather than later.

'So, how did you find the fossils, Mitch?'

He responded immediately and with warmth while vigorously stirring his tea. 'I'd been out mustering sheep on the quad bike and was heading back here to the homestead doing the waters on the way when one of the front wheels hit something. I stopped to check it out and got excited.'

At Mitch's mention of doing the waters, she knew he meant checking the stock wells and bores all over a big station like this.

The enthusiasm on his face and in his smooth deep voice made him look like a kid who had just received a new toy. 'How did you know it was special?'

'This boy has been bringing home rocks and stones all his life,' Ed said with gruff fondness and a chuckle.

Father and son shared a grin making their deep bond plain.

'Pretty much just a hunch so I went back next day and poked around. Found more. Bigger.'

'I'd like to have a look at the real things soon, if possible.'

'Sure.' He nodded and sipped his tea. 'What happens next?'

'After I've seen the fossils and can confirm the observations we made back at the museum from your photographs, I'd like to head out to the site and set up camp before we lose daylight.'

'You're welcome to stay here overnight and Mitch can take you out tomorrow,' Nina chipped in.

Darcy glanced out the kitchen window at the gathering dusk. 'Thanks all the same but I'd prefer to be on site, check it out at first light and get ahead of the field team arriving tomorrow. I need to map out the exact position where Mitch found the larger pieces and set up a grid where they'll probably need to start digging. It's likely we'll find concentrations of smaller bones.'

Mitch eyed Darcy across the table again. 'I've driven a front end loader out there already so you can tell me where to start digging off the top soil when you've marked it out.'

'Great. You've done this before.'

'I've volunteered on other digs. Not on our station though.'

'Since this whole region of central Queensland is dinosaur country it was only a matter of time,' Darcy said. 'Judging by our initial investigations from your images, it's looking like yours is another sauropod, one of the plant eating dinosaurs.'

Nina finished her tea in a generous gulp and crossed her arms before her. 'How on earth did a gorgeous woman like you get interested in dinosaurs?'

Darcy's lips edged into a nostalgic smile.

'Hard not to, really, the way my brothers and I were raised. Our Grandpa Joe was a park ranger in the Territory. He respected and learnt from the aboriginals at a time when many ignorantly believed them primitive. He collected all kinds of stuff and, I guess, sort of passed on his passion to me. He took me to a museum in Darwin and I never recovered,' she admitted with a shrug and laughed.

Mitch's appreciative gaze drifted over her and settled.

Trying to ignore him, she continued, 'He took us out in the bush and we lived rough. He loved wide open spaces. Hated boundaries and fences. Said it made him feel hemmed in. And country music?' Darcy was deep in reminiscence. 'Never heard anyone turn it up louder on the radio.' Embarrassed at her ramblings, she hesitated. 'He's gone now, of course.'

'Sounds like my kind of man,' Ed reached out and gently laid a hand on her arm.

'One of a kind,' Darcy said softly.

'Where's home for you?' Nina asked.

'Brisbane at the moment but I'm from Darwin originally.'

Darcy twinged with annoyance at feeling compelled to move from the Territory. Despite her private reasons, with all the fossil discoveries in outback Queensland, it made sense to transfer her work here. At least for now.

'Family?' Nina was saying with genuine

womanly interest.

'My parents Dave and Laura still live up there. Dad's an environmental scientist. Six months of the year in the winter dry season he's a tour guide based on an outback station. In the Wet, he teaches in Darwin. My oldest brother Andy works on big cattle station properties and young Joe Junior is a chef and owns a café in Darwin.'

'We have lots of friends in the Territory,' Ed said. 'Haven't been to visit in a while.'

'And whose fault is that, working seven days?' Nina teased, rising from the table. 'We should let Mitch show Darcy his finds while I scare up some food to go for her until the crew arrives in the morning. Then while he takes her out to the waterhole, Ed Beaumont you have paperwork waiting in the office.'

'We'll take a run out in the morning,' Ed said to Darcy, pressing a hand gently on her shoulder as he passed and disappeared down the hall.

Nina bustled about the kitchen and Mitch moved around the table. 'Follow me,' he said to Darcy, leading her through closed French doors which he slid open at the far end of the kitchen, revealing the generous family living area she had glimpsed from the hall on their way in.

'Wow. Impressive,' Darcy breathed, planting her hands on her hips and shaking her head.

'Kind of a family collection,' Mitch murmured beside her. Darcy didn't need to look at him to know he was smiling. 'Dad started and we've both added to it ever since.'

The entire wall before them was glass fronted shelved cabinets crammed with specimens, stones, even some rare and unique boulder opal, still imprisoned in its rock, glittering and colourful beneath the special cupboard down lighting inside.

'I see your latest babies.' She peered closer, recognising the pieces from his emailed images to the museum.

Mitch opened the cabinet to retrieve them then slid out a concealed shelf and flicked on an overhead light so Darcy could professionally examine them firsthand.

'May I?' Mitch nodded. Darcy reverently nestled them in her hand. 'Every time I pick up something like this I still find it hard to believe its millions of years old.' She slowly turned it over to study. 'Definitely skull fragments. Here's hoping we find more of the skeleton like maybe teeth and other bones, even ribs if its complete enough.' She looked across at him. 'The paddock where you found these is going to look like a bomb site for a few weeks,' she warned.

Mitch shrugged. 'I know. That's cool. This is exciting for us on the station. Whatever you need.'

'Thanks.' She glanced outside through more French doors that led out onto the veranda. 'We're losing light. Mind if we make tracks?'

Mitch nodded, replaced the fossil fragments, turned off the lights and stepped aside. 'I'll lead the way.'

Which was a top idea since Darcy was having trouble concentrating. Normally she was fully absorbed when her mind settled into work mode but her mental distraction had nothing to do with being weary and she was annoyed with herself for not being more professional.

This man was the cause, practically rubbing shoulders and standing so close. No ring on his finger; not that bush men always wore one and he clearly lived in the homestead. No sign of a partner in his life, at least out here on the property. Women hereabouts must be positively panting over this bloke. Darcy knew a flick of envy that some local female might have the annoying good fortune to be a part of his life.

On the veranda, they both put on their boots again.

Striding down the path to the front fence toward her bike, Mitch rattled a bunch of keys and nodded to the road leading in. 'I'll meet you on the track. Dig site's a few miles out near that far line of coolabahs following the creek to the waterhole.'

'See you out there.'

Darcy slid on her leather jacket, grabbed her helmet and gloves. Geared up and with her bike humming beneath her again, she rumbled to the track and waited. Dust announced Mitch's approach in a ute from the direction of a machinery shed. His lazy wave as he passed, arm resting on the open window, bumped Darcy's mood higher.

Next few weeks should prove interesting.

Chapter 2

Mitch enjoyed the early evening breeze drifting in from the ute's open window as it tossed his hair. His brows and thoughts deepened under his broad hat, eyes automatically scouring the flat landscape for anything unusual. He drove to one side of the track.

A glance in the rear view mirror told him the female rider behind understood why and was riding on the opposite side to avoid his dusty trail. She was one cruisy chick. Confident and clearly self-sufficient. A fellow outback spirit. A younger version of his own tiny but determined mother.

The long ends of Darcy's dark hair were flying out behind her from under the helmet, those long shapely legs not completely innocent packed tight as they were inside those jeans. If he didn't concentrate he would be driving off the road and looking like an idiot.

She wasn't exactly skinny. More like lean and loose limbed. Moved easily. Was fit. Whether she was looking at you or talking, her smooth chocolate eyes sparked with life. But she had revealed a vulnerable side when she'd spoken of her grandfather. Family was important to her yet he sensed a lost and drifting soul buried deep. One way or another, he figured everyone was a casualty moulded by life's path so far. Be interesting to know Darcy Manning's personal struggle.

His own was a carefree and reckless older brother and heir, Hartley, destined to inherit *Matilda Downs*. If he wanted it. Mitch knew himself to be biased and single hearted about this country. He loved it with a deep and fierce pride but Hart didn't.

As a backup, in case Hart changed his mind, surprised the hell out of everyone and chose to stay on the family property, probably bringing in a manager, Mitch had acquired his own patch of dirt with a timber cottage further west along the foothills of the jump up. Part of it had been leased by his father which he bought when the lease ran out and the bloke running his cattle on agistment didn't renew. The rest he had acquired as a chunk on the far edge boundary of a neighbouring station.

Personally, Mitch couldn't see Hart hanging around. His moody brother was too restless. He'd never settle out here. Sooner rather than later, one morning he would just be gone. Mitch had long ago decided to stick around on the home place until the property issue and family situation was sorted. His parents sometimes joked about *retirement* then sobered with the truth of knowing neither wanted to leave the land they both loved.

Mitch knew his folks worried over Hart's lack of dedication or interest in running the station. He was away more than in residence. The whole family knew what should be done but it was hard for Ed and Nina to sit down with everyone and actually confront the decision.

Christopher or Kit as he was always known, the third Beaumont child and youngest son was a born salesman. The perfect marketing guru for their station business. He did the books, struck deals with his casual manner and easy smile, often travelling to Asia to set up new or extended livestock markets for the station. Which is where he was right now. He was happy to help run *Matilda Downs* alongside his father but, long term, everyone was tapping their feet waiting for Hart's decision.

Personally, Mitch thought Ed should push it but the old man was giving his first born a long rope and biding time. Their father's patience was legendary but with every passing year, Mitch was growing frustrated over the inaction and would have hustled Hart years ago. After a lifetime on the land and reading people well, Ed believed in signs and fate. Everything for a reason but making wise decisions in-between.

Their little sister Elise was such a talented

artist, Mitch would swear her paintings were photographs. They were *that* detailed and real. Perfectly capturing her native landscape. Even as a skinny little kid happily trailing after her older brothers all over the station, she was always scribbling and drawing.

At present, Elise was making her own way, studying at university in Brisbane but Mitch couldn't see her in the city longer than necessary. She would be back.

Somehow, amid his deep thoughts, the ute had found its own way to one of the rare and isolated permanent waterholes on the station surrounded by mulga and fed by creeks that spread out like veins across the country.

Mitch braked beneath the sheltering gums at the edges of its muddy brown waters. As he stepped from the vehicle, he was drawn to its shores by the croaking calls of a flock of black cormorants that swam and played. Waterbirds usually gathered at sunrise and sundown. One flapped its shiny wide wings and settled on a dead tree branch nearby, sheltered by grassy reeds.

He squinted westward. This time of day the lowering sun spread reflections and shadows across its watery surface. He used to paddle a canoe down here as a kid. Spend precious spare hours fishing with Ed and Kit, Hart usually scooting around the property on his mini bike instead, preferring a bit more excitement. Not so much adventure as speed and thrills.

'A beautiful spot.'

Mitch spun around at Darcy's soft observation, realising she had arrived and left her bike to come stand beside him. One hand on a hip, the other combing through her dark silky hair, its ends lifted by the breeze drifting in off the water.

With him sunk in thought, she'd probably been alongside for minutes. She was one striking woman. Contentment played over her face.

'Special for sure,' he murmured.

'And I get to camp here?' she smiled in amused disbelief.

He nodded. 'I'll help you set up.'

'Nah, thanks anyway. I have my tent. And your mum's food. Don't want to keep you from anything. You must have heaps to do.'

'Not at this time of day.'

She cast her gaze around the vicinity and asked, 'Okay if I light a fire?'

'I'll grab some firewood.'

Darcy knew real gentlemen were a rare breed. Especially out here. Men needed to be tough. Mitch Beaumont managed to combine physical ruggedness with a damned appealing healthy dose of very sexy charm. She tried hard not to stare when she arrived but with his back turned and frowning out across the waterhole, Mitch was clearly distracted and absorbed in his own world.

Before he had registered her presence, she had a moment to admire the scowl, soft mouth, appealing shadow of stubble on his chin and utter stillness of such a big physical man. Bit of a turn on really. Then she remembered why she was here and this was work. No entanglements or distractions, Darcy. This field trip and every other had an underlying purpose. Until that brought results and her mission was done, she needed to stay focused. And single. Although an occasional night with a decent bloke never went amiss.

This bloke ticked pretty much every box. She watched his arm muscles flex and legs and butt tighten as he bent to collect kindling, snapping heavier branches in half with ease for her fire. Its warmth and comfort would be welcome when night and temperatures fell soon. Already a crisp chill lingered in the air.

Darcy hauled her camping pack from the bike closer to the water. When Mitch dropped a huge bundle of wood she couldn't resist asking, 'Which direction is the dig site?'

He pointed behind her. 'Few hundred metres that way.'

Her enthusiasm buzzed. 'Might go scope it out.'

She ignored his funny look and strode to find it, her thoughts fantasizing with excitement at what might be just below the top soil. When she reached it, for now the dig site was just like any other patch of spinifex grassland except for patches of the area lightly turned over by Mitch's obvious scouting around and his front end loader parked to one side.

She likened this familiar expectant feeling to being let loose on a scavenger hunt in a giant sandpit. She certainly always felt the same childish sense of promise every time a new dig was about to get underway. The suspense never dulled.

Tomorrow this site would come alive with the arrival of the field crew and equipment trailers and vehicles from Winton when the work and discovery and friendship would begin.

Most helpers would be enthusiastic volunteers. Everyone would know their place and job on site, Darcy would oversee and catalogue their finds in her own small open-sided tent, carefully labelling even the tiniest fragment before it was sealed in a plastic bag and transported back to the lab.

The camp cook would set up in a large open-sided catering tent, and the sieving cradle and tables with piped water hoses would be near the site for screening the dirt.

Then it would be all crew down on hands and knees sorting and digging. Not glamorous but the process and anticipation of possible finds grabbed you like a bug. Absorbed, it was Darcy's turn to be surprised, suddenly dragged from pre-dig fever at the sound of Mitch's heavy boots behind. She turned at his approach.

His gaze wandered over her with warm amusement, a playful smile on his mouth. 'Great to see a fellow enthusiast.'

Darcy shrugged. 'It's in the blood.' She looked across the site. 'We'll see how much more of your guy we find out there.'

'Like to be a part of it.'

Scary thought. Mitch Beaumont around all day. She covered her confusion with humour and details. 'You'll be assured of a job. When more than a few bones are found together and appear to be from the same dinosaur, we dig. Since you've already done that, it will be all systems go in the morning.' She rubbed her bare arms against the chill. 'What fossils may or may not lie here represent not just the region but our whole country.'

'It's getting cool. You should light that fire.'

As they sauntered back to the waterhole, Darcy was surprised to note an unexpected glow of kinship with Mitch's boyish intensity. He was equally passionate about his finds. This intangible bond among fossil hunters she normally only encountered with fellow colleagues or a particular selective fraternity of devoted digger enthusiasts.

Back at camp, Darcy pulled up short. 'You've erected my tent.' And built a fire ready to light for the evening.

'Figured you might be a while over there.'

He dismissed her pleased reaction as though his thoughtful actions were something he did every day. Having only met him today, she suspected he probably did. No doubt a combination of his awesome nature and how he had been raised.

'Well, thanks.'

'Sure you'll be okay out here?'

Darcy grinned as he hovered, clearly reluctant to leave. She folded her arms. 'Positive. You've put up my tent and set the fire. I've camped on my own a few times before and it's only for one night,' she reminded him. 'Crew will be out tomorrow. I want to make an early start on mapping out the dig area in the morning before they arrive.'

'I'll swing by early so you can tell me where you want to start removing dirt.'

'Around your find area for starters and we'll work out from there.'

'Rug up tonight. It's going to be chilly.' He hesitated. 'Might be wise to give you my mobile number. For emergency contact,' he added in justification, almost like an excuse.

'Makes sense. Should have suggested we swap them myself.'

Darcy acted casual and pushed down on the small thrill of pleasure and reassurance it gave her to tap his name and number into her contact list. Moments later, she watched him stroll and drive away, the ute's red tail lights growing smaller, finally disappearing into the night altogether.

She knew a dash of disappointment that quickly vanished knowing he would be back in the morning. Best get some beauty sleep then. She lit the fire and settled on the ground munching through Nina's picnic meal and pouring a hot mug of tea when the billy sang to a boil.

Snuggled into her leather jacket with a beanie pulled down over her hair and ears, watching leaping orange flames, Darcy let the brisk night air and all its accompanying sounds of nesting wildlife surround and lull her back into the familiar contentment that surfaced whenever she returned to the outback again.

Flicks of first light through the canvas and the sharp laugh of a kookaburra echoing in the bush brought Darcy awake. She climbed from her sleeping bag, still fully dressed and unzipped the tent flap. A thin veil of low mist clung to the surface of the waterhole and sharp pale sunlight sparkled on its waters.

She stood up and stretched, kicked the fire back into life with more wood, then sat half in and out of her tent opening eating a bowl of cereal while the billy boiled again. As she cupped her cold hands around the warm mug, Darcy's lively thoughts already raced ahead to the necessary speed and efficiency of organising the dig site ready for the volunteers.

Today would be set up day but there was no time to waste. While they would all be here to work, the days themselves brought their own rewarding reveals, the nights around the campfire with camaraderie, laughter and stories would be a memorable highlight for everyone before the weary bunch retired to rest for another day's labour of love.

Darcy finished breakfast, made her camp fire safe and walked over to the dig site taking photos on her phone to email back to the museum. She was marking out the initial site perimeter when the sound of a distant motor and a light cloud of dust signalled the return of a familiar ute. This time with passengers and one of the dogs she had met yesterday in the back.

It leapt out and raced toward her. 'Good morning. You're early.' She fondled its ears.

She straightened to greet all three. Mitch was already striding closer, Ed holding the ute door open for Nina who both followed. *That's where Mitch gets it from*, the thought slipped into Darcy's mind. His father's respectful gesture out here in the middle of nowhere stirred a deep longing in Darcy. Flickers of memory surfaced when she recalled her father performing a similar courtesy many times for her mother. She shut down an unfamiliar ache, a sense of something missing, and smiled at the visitors' approach.

Ed and Nina were rugged up in padded parkas. The first chill of morning would soon burn off as the sun strengthened but Mitch braved it in a quilted vest over wranglers and shirt sleeves rolled back above his wrists.

'Sleep okay?' he asked softly, his gaze on her from beneath the brim of his hat tugged low.

Darcy nodded. 'Ready for work?'

'Absolutely.'

'Morning young lady,' Ed greeted.

'Darcy.' Nina smiled warmly. 'Going to be an exciting time on *Matilda*.'

'For sure. If your son,' she flicked a gaze at Mitch, 'wouldn't mind jumping into the loader and excavate the soil at that top end where he found the biggest fossils, I'd be obliged.'

'On it.'

Mitch leapt into the machine, firing it up and starting work. Carefully, she noted. If he had been on other digs he would know the process. Being a fellow addict, she trusted his judgement and appreciated his eagerness to help. Seemed he was as keen as her to make a start.

His parents stood aside watching with genuine interest, keeping the frisky dog mostly under control at their side.

By mid-morning, Darcy was surveying and scratching around where Mitch had worked. He'd cut the machine and was alongside her chipping away at the soil near his recent finds. Once the field team arrived, progress would be faster. For now, she forgot everything as they dug except brushing shoulders with Mitch, watching his strong tanned arms and hands as they worked together.

'I have a good feeling about this,' Darcy murmured, intent on her task, her long hair tied back for work.

'Me too,' Mitch said in a deep measured tone loaded with suggestion. She didn't need his quick glance and grin to interpret the double meaning. Darcy had meant fossils, of course, but she sensed Mitch was talking about something else entirely. Her body warmed with awareness.

'You two should stop for smoko,' Nina called out. 'I have scones and a thermos on the ute tray.'

Mitch cleared his throat and rose, holding out a hand to help Darcy. She didn't need it but accepted and his big rough hand clamped around hers, pulling her up.

'We should wash up.' Darcy stepped away from him, needing to create distance, not usually afraid of anything but this man left her unsettled and intrigued.

'Dad keeps a water container in the back of the ute.'

'Finding anything else yet?' Nina asked as the two diggers joined them.

'A bit soon,' Darcy grinned, 'but it looks promising.'

Mitch hunkered down nearby, his back

resting against a ute tyre, gulping hot tea and demolishing scones, the dog companionably stretched out beside him.

Nina and Ed wandered the newly disturbed site, their chatty but indistinct murmurs floating back to the ute.

Anxious about the vibes of attraction from Mitch, as much as she liked the man, Darcy hoped he didn't come out here every day as he indicated earlier. He was keen on both her and the dig that was plain – and truth to tell she was more than a little attracted to the man herself – but surely he had more than enough other work on the station to keep himself occupied. The distraction he caused in her head and heart was new. She could usually take or leave a bloke but this one was proving harder to ignore.

This was the worst time for a cool country boy to capture her attention and get her flustered. Work was the priority here so she best try and stay the hell out of his way when he was around. She was on Beaumont land working for the Museum so from now on she better fix her mind to the job and knuckle down.

'Need more ground shifted with the loader?' Mitch broke their loaded silence.

Darcy shook her head. 'We have enough area exposed to make a start. When the crew arrive and digging is underway, we'll have a better idea of the extent of your find. With good luck and based on what you've already found, we should uncover not only bone clusters at a similar depth from the same skeleton but also more and possibly larger fossils further down.'

'Fingers crossed then.' He rose, gathered up their tin tea mugs and packed up his mother's picnic hamper.

Wow. Sexy *and* domesticated. This man was too good to be true but Darcy didn't have time to dwell on his attributes any longer. As if conjured up from the very words she had spoken only moments before, the field team convoy began arriving.

Nina, Ed and Mitch hung around as people tumbled from a minivan, various vehicles and four wheel drives, some pulling trailers, all of them bearing smiles of excitement, clearly either experienced or prepared for work in tough sensible work clothes, boots and wide brimmed hats.

Judging by the friendship already forged, and echoes of muted laughter disturbing the still country air, they had also brought a sense of humour. Clearly not only Darcy knew they would need it. Some of them, fondly known as *duggers*, had done this before. After greetings and introductions, Darcy directed proceedings and her small work shelter was set up with her laptop, a table and a chair so she could study and log the pieces as they were found.

The catering tent was erected further back where their cook, Dawnie, would prepare all meals which included hot breakfasts plus morning and afternoon tea break, or *smoko* as it was known out here.

The tools and supply vehicles and trailers were parked at the site's edge while the sieving table was set up a short distance back.

The Beaumonts hung around, keenly interested not just to watch this unfolding potential thrill of discovery on their station but actually pitching in to help, embracing and sharing Ed and Mitch's obvious underlying passion.

Around midday they waved and all left in the ute. Darcy felt a sense of loss for Mitch's departure but realised she could now settle down without any sense of diversion.

Darcy's personal excitement rose. All day she answered questions and gave guidance. Most diggers simply picked their spot and started looking, hoping to bring ancient history to life by dusting off bone bits of a monster millions of years old from the past.

By the end of the first day, the volunteers, sleeves rolled up and digging in the warm winter sun, were actually beginning to expose more fossil material, having been taught to differentiate bone fragments from rock.

It was a slow painstaking process but always with the dream of reward. For Darcy though this potential new discovery came with reservations. Word of any exciting find would spread among the dinosaur community and with it, always lay the threat of invasion and potential smuggling. Of which she had endured an unpleasant firsthand experience

She winced with bad memories. If this dig proved significant, which she suspected, the temptation for people - and one man in particular - may prove too great to resist. She could only hope not and press on, taking every precaution and remaining vigilant. Hopefully keeping their isolated dig site confidential would help.

At the close of the first day's dig, everyone took grateful turns under the solar shower and soaked up another glorious outback sunset, sipping their beer and drinks. Now all satisfied since devouring Dawnie's substantial evening meal and sitting around the communal camp fire, all glances turned casually toward the approaching sound of a vehicle engine in the dark and its headlights piercing the night.

A short time later, Mitch strolled toward them from the shadows. 'Evening all.'

Many acknowledged him by name or a casual wave. Clearly locals.

'Boss,' someone quipped wryly and laughter rippled around the group.

'We found the rest of your dinosaur, mate!'

'Did we?' a man chuckled. 'Great. I won't be stiff anymore and we can all go home, then.'

Friendly banter continued until Mitch edged

closer around the fire to Darcy. They had been watching each other around the group, trying not to appear obvious but the call between them was strong. Darcy cursed. She didn't need this now.

Mitch squatted down beside her. 'So what did you find today?'

Deciding for more reasons than one, she needed to get him aside, she asked, 'Want to come have a look?'

Mitch nodded, Darcy rose and she led him over to her work tent.

Chapter 3

Once Darcy and Mitch had strolled a distance from the field team, relaxed and chatting about today's finds, and the campfire light faded into gloom behind them, she revealed the day's fossil finds to him that she had separated into boxes on the table in her tent. He gave a low whistle of appreciation picking up pieces and turning them over in his hands.

'The team will be working much longer on excavating the bigger bones we're finding, part of a skull and vertebrae. Once we've isolated them they'll need a plaster cap. Depending on final size, we'll need your digger to help lift them out.

'We might even be justified in digging a test hole to see if there's more bone at depth. But at the moment the skeleton layout is spreading horizontal. It's a fragmented but identifiable almost complete top half. Very rare. Once we've dug out more we'll know the exact extent and dimensions. A few of the more experienced duggers in the team are working on revealing a skull. Everyone is so excited.'

Darcy paused in her enthusiasm beneath Mitch's soft gaze of admiration.

'So I can see,' he said warmly. 'Sounds promising.'

'If it's as substantial as it appears and since it's a new find, we'll give it a name. How does *Mitch* sound?'

He threw his head back and laughed.

'You discovered him,' Darcy shrugged and melted inside at the boyish joy on his face and his natural easy mood. He was satisfying to be around. As the moment ebbed between them, she lowered her voice to a murmur although at this distance she doubted anyone else could overhear.

'This dig is shaping up to stretch much further into the centre of the area we've already dug. As I said, what we're seeing appears to be substantial remains.' She held his gaze so he knew the importance of what she was saying. 'Every dig we hope to find more sauropods to establish how many different species co-existed. This new skeleton discovery has the potential to blow us away and be staggering on this specific site. You've stumbled onto a massive scientific find.'

Darcy warmed to her subject but didn't want to bore Mitch even though he was of a similar mind and equally enthusiastic.

'So, what you're saying is another old man

dinosaur is out there just waiting to be found, huh?'

'Yeah, simple as that,' Darcy quipped wryly.

She tried to make light of the situation but hesitated to mention the potential risk of such a precious discovery being stolen and smuggled out of the country to some filthy rich collector with no regard for its inestimable value.

She reflected on whether or not to express and raise her concerns at this early stage of their dig, confide her suspicions and fears, informing Mitch of her background knowledge and past issues with dig site raids. Although it had been his discovery on his family's station property, with the necessary permit in place to explore further, it was now a museum operation under her leadership. So what to do? Inform him now of her personal predicament or maybe confide at a later date or not at all?

Prompted by an urge and trust she couldn't explain, her need to share won out and she said slowly, 'I know the field crew will be tactful about being on the brink of another really vital discovery but could I also suggest that you and your family be cautious about the dig location and keep our findings private.'

Mitch scowled. 'So you're saying Mum's the word?'

Darcy sighed and paced. 'Let's just say at this stage I have serious concerns and we need to take every precaution. In one way our isolation out here is an advantage but it can also be a downfall. So a couple of the men have agreed to share night patrols.'

'Fair enough. I realise fossil finds are of great importance but can you give me any specific reason?'

'A hunch...and a bad past encounter.'

He leant back against the table, crossed his arms and legs and studied her intently. 'Care to elaborate?'

He was pressing and quite frankly Darcy was reluctant to divulge details, afraid of losing Mitch's regard. After all, every situation, even with all the facts, was open to each person's interpretation and personal truth. He may think her prejudiced. Besides, she had no current evidence yet on this site. It was early days. They had only just begun but her exposure to the lengths these powerful people would manipulate to get what they wanted kept her edgy.

'Not just yet. It may all come to nothing and prove I'm just being paranoid. At the moment, call it intuition but I'd prefer not to ignore it. For now I can only ask you to trust me. The dig team and museum staff already know, of course, and a few other restricted professionals in the science world but if you could pass the word onto your family I would appreciate it.'

Following Darcy's urgent plea, Mitch's concentrated gaze let her know he took on board her unease. 'You believe this dig site and any further unearthed fossils are really at risk?'

She shrugged. 'Always possible. I'm just asking that everyone involved remain diplomatic and guarded.'

Darcy wasn't ready to explain her position and appear foolish when her fears might come to nothing and all could turn out well. She could only hope. But since that matter five years ago as an enthusiastic and naïve graduate she had innocently stumbled close to the bitter truth. That a fellow experienced scientist who she had looked up to could use the knowledge and control of a dig for personal financial gain, ignoring every moral code of their profession. Asking too many questions, getting too close and daring to voice the possibility of fossil smuggling, she had been swiftly and efficiently ridiculed and legally silenced as a result. And oddly, although now she was more informed, most digs ever since on which she had been the leading scientist had somehow been compromised and interference or drama followed.

Darcy no longer wondered about a conspiracy to guarantee her *cooperation*. She was a target and no mistake. Her opponent and his bosses had made it plain they clearly sought retribution because she had dared to be outspoken all those years ago and tried to keep her under control against the threat of exposing their cosy little inside operation.

They were intent on pressure at the very least, the risk of damage if not the total destruction of her career in the process. She didn't care for her own safety – whatever it took to achieve a result. Darcy just wanted to outsmart and expose them but she always prayed no one else was endangered in the process. This was her mission alone. Her enemies had made it that way so she would shrewdly continue to trail them and never give up until her suspicions were confirmed and she gathered enough proof so justice was served.

'Are you in personal danger?' Mitch murmured with such genuine concern and protective warmth, his gaze probing, she was almost moved to tears.

So far she had fought this battle secretly and alone, working under a professional cloud. It was heartening to even have the possibility of another person in her corner. Mitch Beaumont would be worth having alongside on her mission. He was a man's man. It was clear he could handle himself in any situation but Darcy suddenly felt afraid for his safety, even by the most tenuous association with her so far.

Darcy blinked hard against her emotions, usually never given rein. 'I doubt it will come to that.'

As a precaution she had documented everything so far, her papers and diaries securely locked away. Just in case. But of course she hoped the situation never descended to anywhere near such a chilling scenario.

Mitch made a move which triggered Darcy's focus again. 'Sure you don't want me to stay?'

Now there was a leading question. 'I'll be fine.'

'I certainly hope so,' he drawled, brushing past her to leave the tent, the brief touch tingling all her senses. 'Tomorrow.'

'See you then.' She folded her arms, inhaled deeply to steady her tension and after tidying her specimen table, followed at a discreet distance a short time later.

As Mitch strolled away, waving goodnight to those still remaining around the campfire and heading back to his ute, Darcy's compelling thoughts tracked back to the worries on her mind.

She still had to work out the one single connection that tied each of her previous suspicious dig invasions together. At least with every passing day on every excavation field site, that solution loomed closer. The last one had proven nasty, resulting in veiled threats. Central outback Queensland was dinosaur country so her professional options to move were limited to this area. Having gained more insight by some tricky undercover surveillance work, she had backed off but the identity of the top culprit driving the crimes was only one small slip away from discovery. She had learned that patience was a worthy virtue and waited.

Problem was, she was in their sights. Whoever *they* were. Somehow, some way, they would be watching. This time, on *Matilda Downs* so far, the discovery and location to a degree was temporarily secure to those immediately involved. What she only hoped to restrict was wider knowledge. But the entire Beaumont family and all the lovely innocent volunteers among the field crew were at risk so Darcy felt a heavy responsibility to protect them all and knew to stay vigilant.

Mitch drove back to the homestead, arm resting on the open ute window. The Doc was getting under his skin and not only because of her dig site security concerns.

She feared something potentially illegal which put her in danger. Maybe it was the way she had left her hair down tonight, usually caught back and pinned under a cap during the day on the dig, spilling around her shoulders it had made her look so soft and vulnerable he had wanted to stick around for protection.

But the underlying steel beneath that curvy exterior revealed a country woman who would probably handle herself in most situations. He only hoped if it came right down to it he would be around for those times she couldn't. Something was niggling her and he would make it his business to find out exactly what. But he would need to earn her confidence first. Darcy Manning was one wary sweetheart so it would be vital to get his timing right.

As he passed the homestead, its warm welcoming lights blazing from its French doors, to put the ute in the shed for the night, Mitch groaned. A shiny black American GMC pickup with a bull bar and the overkill of way too many headlights, spotlights and aerials, was parked in front of the house. Bloody Hartley was back. Where the hell had he been the past few days when he was needed out here for lambing?

If his big brother decided to take on this station and then let it rot through disinterest and poor management, on behalf of not just his parents and their whole family but also his ancestors who had built this property by hard toil, he would be answering to one outraged little brother.

As Mitch garaged his vehicle, strode across the yard and leapt the front steps up onto the veranda, he prepared for a confrontation. Guaranteed to happen. Hart would either have been drinking or angry about something.

He heard voices and found his parents and errant brother in the sitting room. Already filled with a tension in the air you could slice, the family fell silent when he entered. Mitch also smelt something that incensed him on behalf of his mother, a scrupulous homemaker.

Hart had his back turned as he spoke. 'Just been hearing about the trespassers on the property,' he growled.

Shit, Mitch privately cursed. There goes Darcy's plan for discretion. Hart's big mouth would see to that.

'If you mean the museum volunteers, you're right. They arrived today.'

Mitch moved further into the room to stand facing his brother, arms comfortably crossed and legs apart, letting him know he would never be intimidated.

'Why wasn't I told they were coming?' Hart rose slowly and stepped closer, a threatening scowl on his face and a lit cigar between his fingers.

'You weren't around when we discussed it.' Mitch glanced across to his parents and raised his eyebrows. Understanding, Ed briefly dipped his head and his mother tossed her younger son a look of frustrated tolerance. 'But I'm sure you already know that.' He nodded to Hart's hands. 'Have a little respect for our mother. Either put that thing out or take it outside.'

Nina would have already asked but rather more politely.

Hart ignored his brother's suggestion. 'You should have waited until I was here.'

'We're not always sure when that will be, bro. The museum could only excavate in the current two week time frame. They don't work to the whims of an idle station owner's son and his unreliable appearances.'

Hart's black glare told him he'd pushed it with his low verbal blow but in recent times there seemed little in common between the two older brothers. Hart had taken advantage of his little brother's loyalty when they were young but the boy had long ago wised up. Not anymore.

'You should have phoned to get my permission,' he snarled.

'No need. Father owns this property and he gave it,' Mitch said with harnessed cool but growing tense enough to snap.

Hart drew long on his cigar and deliberately blew the smoke straight at his brother. 'We don't know these people. They're trespassing.'

'No they're not.' Mitch stepped aside from the smoke haze closer to his parents. 'It's all legal, as I'm sure Dad has already told you. They have the necessary permit and despite what you think, they're reputable people doing important work.'

Thinking of Darcy and uneasy for her, Mitch's irritation grew. For days he had been out all over the station both with Ed and alone, checking newborn lambs, helping setting up the dig site with no chance to get out to his own property and work on some final renovations to his cottage.

Meeting Darcy had been like a refreshing

breeze sweeping in. Then Hart returns like he's some kind of welcome gift to everyone and starts challenging decisions made while he was away. None of which he had any right to question and placed their father in an awkward defensive position.

Mitch felt his emotional balance shifting and lost his calm. 'She has a Doctorate for Christ's sake,' he muttered.

He instantly regretted his outburst when Hart picked up on the information and his interest sharpened. 'She?' he scowled.

'The lead palaeontologist. She's one of only a few women in her profession. She knows her stuff.'

So help him, if Hart went anywhere near Darcy he would be right behind him, watching.

Hart whirled on his parents seated together on the sofa. Ed stoically pretending to watch television, Nina flipping magazine pages too quickly to be reading. 'We should stop this. Digging up our land for nothing. This is damn fine grazing country.'

At least his brother knew that much, Mitch mused. 'Too late. It's underway.'

'Been through this with you already, Hart,' Ed sighed. 'Like Mitch said, works already started. Only be here a couple weeks and they're nowhere near any sheep.'

Not that Hart would care about that, Mitch thought.

'Kettle's boiled if you want a cuppa, Mitch,' his mother said, keeping her head down.

Experience had long ago told them to all ignore the first born until he simmered down. Mitch wondered where he went that always riled him up on his return. No use asking. He would never say.

When Hart started a speech presenting with some authority the laws about fossil finds on private land, Mitch raised his eyebrows in amazement. Hart knew his facts? Never much for school and education, Mitch wondered where he had acquired them.

'Didn't know you were interested in fossils,' he baited.

'I'm not,' Hart retorted. 'I'm also not the dumb ass you all think I am.'

He drew another long puff of his cigar and stalked from the house, no doubt to sulk in the cottage he used nearby on the station whenever he was around.

Mitch and his parents shared confused glances and then his brain ticked into overdrive with suspicion. Since boyhood, Mitch had been awestruck when his father returned to the homestead to share the bits of fossils he'd stumbled upon all over *Matilda Downs*. So over the years it became family lore and understanding that these finds were legally the property of the collector. But Hart had never shown any interest. Now, suddenly he knew details?

For this first dig of any significance on the station, Ed had already agreed and signed the papers necessary that any finds would become part of the Museum's collection. Where the family all considered they rightly belonged, to be preserved for all time. Apparently except Hart,

From a lifetime's interest in fossils since that first discovery as a boy, Mitch knew dinosaurs were on this land first, roaming the swampy forests of the area as it had been back then hundreds of millions of years ago. He agreed with professionals like Darcy on the importance of studying and placing them in the big scheme of evolution, adding knowledge to the still-unfolding story of life on earth. Before the gigantic magnificent beasts and three quarters of all plants and animals had been destroyed in a mass extinction by that one cataclysmic event over sixty million years ago.

Mitch continued to puzzle over why the hell Hart was only now showing interest in dinosaurs. It didn't figure. At least according to his brother's track record of past indifference.

Beyond cups of tea at this hour, Mitch snapped open a can of beer from the fridge and returned to join his long-suffering parents in the lounge. Taking a seat, he knocked down a few refreshing mouthfuls and set the can on the central wooden table between them. He leaned forward, hands clasped between his legs.

'Wish I'd returned sooner.' Although he could never regret a single moment spent with Darcy Manning. 'Ironically just before I left the dig site earlier, the Doc expressed her concerns that she wanted us to be careful about sharing too much info. Looks like being a decent find out there. Believe she's just being cautious,' he underplayed Darcy's request out on site but knew it came from genuine intuition. 'All the same,' he added.

'We could never have kept it from Hart.' Nina laid down her magazine with a sigh.

'No but he'd blab even if we warned him not to,' Ed said quietly.

'And likely stir up trouble,' Mitch added.

They all nodded and fell silent while Mitch enjoyed his beer again.

'Might do another run around the paddocks. Check on any new lambs,' he said eventually.

He wouldn't sleep much anyway since Darcy's warning tonight and Hart's disapproval and resentment complicating matters no end. Nothing new but because of his attitude the family's future situation had to be tackled.

'Leave it till the morning, son,' Ed said.

Mitch shrugged. 'Promised Darcy I'd help on the site for a while.' He ran a weary hand over his face.

Ed rose to his feet, frowned and paced. 'Need to make a decision about the station's future.

Never seems the right time to raise the topic but Hart's behaviour and attitude is getting impossible to deal with. I'll set up an appointment with our station lawyers and take a run into Longreach. Maybe do an overnighter. What do you say, my dear?' He turned a loving gaze toward Nina.

'Sounds like a plan, Ed. It's time.'

He nodded sagely. 'Afraid so. Disappointed it's come to this.'

'We all are, Dad.'

Before he left the room, Ed turned back to his son. 'I know you have your own station property now but your mother and I would appreciate it if you could give thought to at least helping here or taking over management in the future.' He placed an arm around his wife's shoulder when she approached, sensitive to the upset this discussion always caused among them. Mitch knew *Matilda Downs* was his father's lifeblood and his mother had been at his side all the way.

'I'd be honoured to give it a shot, Dad, you know that. I could work the two properties.'

'With help.'

Mitch chuckled. 'Probably. When Kit comes back from his Asian trip maybe he would be open to some kind of managing partnership.'

'And Elise has to figure in it all, too,' Ed pointed out although the family realised that was a given.

Noticeably there was no mention of Hart. They would all need to accept the decision their parents made. Which would be determined as always after input from everyone and joint family discussions.

'Our daughter loves this country,' Ed went on, 'and my instinct is she'll settle down somewhere out here.'

'She just needs the right man who'll be comfortable with her disappearing off into the bush to paint.' Nina grinned.

'She'll find him,' Mitch said. 'My strong-willed sister knows exactly what she wants.'

'Let's hit the hay, Ed,' Nina said. 'We'll do an early start tomorrow around the sheep while Mitch is at the dig. Maybe we'll join you out there for lunch.'

He nodded. 'It's a date. I'll try not to wake you when I get back.'

'You never do when you stay here,' Nina said kindly, standing on her toes to give her son a hug. 'Maybe look in on Hart in the cottage before you turn in,' she suggested with a hint of indecision.

'Doubt he'll appreciate it but I'll try to be inconspicuous.'

'His door's never locked. Just a quick check. Set our minds at rest.'

Mitch nodded. Being a parent never stopped. Being the responsible younger brother for an irresponsible older sibling came even harder, especially as his parents aged and he stepped in where he could to help them. Frankly, Mitch was sick of his brother's selfish nature. No one ever quite knew what unpredictable Hart would do next.

Elise's blunt honesty didn't stand any nonsense. Out of all of the siblings, even though she was the smallest, she was the one most likely to confront her oldest brother about anything.

Kit mostly ignored Hart and did his own thing but he loved management and marketing and travel so to *Matilda Downs'* advantage, he was often absent with good and mutually agreed reason on station business. He had cruised through his degree at university and now there was a certain likely female in the wings who currently lived and worked in tourism on the Sunshine Coast. Mitch suspected it was simply a matter of convincing the girl of the benefits of living in the outback. He could see Kit and any suitable partner living comfortably in the homestead.

As much as he had loved growing up on *Matilda Downs* with nothing but the fondest memories, Mitch himself was planning on settling down on his own land. Renovate and extend the cottage. He'd love kids somewhere down the track. Like Kit, he just needed to find the right country woman who would be prepared to love and walk beside him in life.

Odd that at that particular moment an image

of Darcy's face and winning smile came into his mind.

Chapter 4

Darcy woke and stretched in her tent to the crisp feel of the morning air and sounds of screeching parrots feeding out on the waterhole and in the gum trees nearby. She had taken a quick bush shower after Mitch left late last night so she pulled on her warm windcheater and boots, knotted a scarf around her neck and strolled over to the catering tent to join the others for breakfast.

Not usually one for more than rushed nourishment since she lived in Brisbane, Darcy noticed her appetite had increased to embarrassing proportions since being in the outback again. Besides, she justified her indulgence because Dawnie's cooking was homely and well presented. Mostly it ran to a bowl of porridge and slabs of toast or scrambled eggs and bacon. A veritable bush feast out here that everyone appreciated, helped along in

Darcy's case by a big mug of tea to kick start her day.

Gradually everyone dispersed to their special place on the dig site, donning hats and smiles, mumbling good naturedly among themselves about stiff knees and rough hands but also with an undercurrent of excitement over what they might uncover for the day.

Murray, a solo grey nomad who had signed up early for the dig and was camping in his own motorhome, returned to his dusty careful work at the sieving table.

For a time, Darcy answered questions, overseeing the team members' work and giving guidance where needed. The expectant atmosphere hummed as fine layers of dirt were either laboriously and meticulously chipped or brushed away, revealing ever more tiny section by tiny section what had lain beneath the topsoil for tens of millions of years.

Even after only one good day's work, *Mitch's* outline and potential shape had been tentatively revealed. Darcy had her fingers crossed that each bone fragment no matter how large or small proved to be another important exposure to add to the growing picture of an animal lying where it had died, undisturbed, only now gradually revealed with the erosion of time. The only clue that such an ancient relic had ever existed.

Darcy still stood in awe sometimes to absorb

the enormity of what was being uncovered.

Thinking of their temporarily named fossil discovery, Darcy's thoughts drifted to the dinosaur skeleton's namesake wondering when he would appear on site as promised last night.

Before she settled to work in her tent for the morning, she strode back to her camp site, drawn by a cloud of dust lingering beyond the trees to the west that usually suggested an approaching vehicle. Mitch already? Her mood lightened.

But it wasn't his now-familiar white ute that came into view. Instead it was a big black beast of a thing travelling, according to Darcy's estimation, way too fast. When the bulky wheels didn't seem to be reducing speed as it grew closer, she quickly leapt aside, heading for the waterhole. Surely the owner of such a flash vehicle had no intention of ending up in the water so she figured she would be safe there.

Just before it finally slewed to a halt, barely metres from her motorbike, campfire and tent, it spat dirt and dust into the air.

Either there was an emergency or the driver was an idiot. Someone else who now knew about the dig site, Darcy's annoyance simmered and she scowled. They better have a damn good explanation for such dangerous driving. She waited, feeling resentful and invaded.

A tanned piece of outback manhood jumped from the ute, slapped a black Akubra low over his forehead to cover a head of sandy hair and strode forward with a big-ass air of authority.

Darcy frowned. Surely not! Blonde. Good looking. Another Beaumont? If so, his attitude was nothing like the rest of the family she had met so far.

'Hartley Beaumont,' he stated with inflated superiority. 'You the boss here?'

She was right! Unbelievable. And the way he introduced himself reeked of self-importance. This blockhead and Mitch were brothers? Confronted by the steamed up male, Darcy's dislike was automatic and instant when he slid his intolerant gaze all over her like she was some kind of female trophy spectacle.

Gritting her teeth against rising indignation, she extended a hand. 'Dr. Darcy Manning. I'm in charge.'

Arrogantly he refused her hand so she let it drop while he ignored her and swaggered about her campsite, circling her pride and joy. Darcy stiffened as he covetously ran his hands over her motor bike.

'This yours?'

She nodded.

'Besides my truck,' he snapped a glance in its direction, 'I own a *decent* powerful ride, too.'

Really? Did she care? Right about now Darcy needed a strong drink and some country music. Both guaranteed to calm her down.

'Does your visit have a purpose, Mr.

Beaumont?' she asked smoothly wishing either one of the men from the dig would come by or Mitch hadn't been delayed.

Darcy had been bullied before so this man's insolence didn't daunt her. But Hartley Beaumont was muscled and built strong. Nudging six feet, Darcy was no pixie but physically this guy was far superior in strength so she would need to stay smart. Strange, Mitch was equally athletic but didn't alarm her in the least.

Her visitor removed a half smoked cigar from his shirt pocket and made a show of striking a match and twirling it as he lit the pungent roll. He covered her with a steady gaze when he blew out the match, flicked it into her fireplace and took his first slow puffs.

The strong smell invaded the surrounding bush. Over this charade, Darcy almost turned her back and walked away. Hartley leaned back against the ute and crossed his legs at the ankles. 'This site is on my property.'

His? No shit.

'I can stop you digging any time.'

He was bluffing of course. Darcy was willing to bet Mitch and his parents knew nothing about this power play. 'Sure, you could try, but we have a permit.'

Hartley scoffed. 'I could challenge that. It's only a piece of paper that could easily get...lost.' He paused while she was supposed to digest his threat, adding, 'So, what are you finding?'

Darcy crossed her arms and played it cool. 'Only been here a few days. Too soon to tell.'

He smirked. 'Question is, would you?'

'I'm sorry?'

Before the conversation deteriorated any further, Darcy closed her eyes in relief at the sight and sound of Mitch's white ute approaching on the winding inward track through the trees. Hartley straightened, looking more pissed off at the interruption than uncomfortable. His little performance was over.

'Great. Maybe now your brother can clear up any…misunderstanding,' Darcy said brightly.

'I'll be back,' Hartley growled as a glowering Mitch left his ute and powered forward.

'Morning,' he pulled up alongside his brother and nodded to both, casting a probing glance to first one then the other.

'Mitch,' Darcy smiled.

'Is there a problem here?'

'Hartley was just-'

'Letting them know to take care,' he cut in.

Hands on hips, Mitch stared his brother down. 'Find it hard to believe you changed your opinion overnight, bro. Ed made a decision. You can accept it or make life harder for yourself and fight it but don't harass this lady again.'

Darcy noticed Mitch's jaw clench tight against the tension stretched between the brothers like a tight fence wire about to snap.

'I come and go on my property as I please. Doctor,' Hart sneered with a curt nod, stuffing the cigar in his mouth, sliding into his truck and speeding away.

'Everything all right here?' Mitch asked with a wrinkled brow of concern.

She nodded. 'Just flexing his muscles.'

'The oldest son and heir,' he pushed out a frustrated sigh. 'Sorry if he was less than polite.'

'I took his measure but, brother or not, if he crosses any line with myself or any of my field team, I'm phoning the police in Winton, okay?' she stated firmly.

'Understood. I know you probably need to get to work but can you take a short break?'

Darcy inclined her head and pushed her hands into her windcheater pockets, curious what he had in mind. 'Sure.'

The desolate call of a crow echoed to them as they strolled down to the water's edge, mirror smooth, casting perfect reflections onto its surface from the overhanging coolabah trees. Mitch gestured and they sat down, legs outstretched, Darcy hugging her knees, Mitch leaning on an elbow idly plucking at grass.

'Hart comes and goes,' Mitch began explaining. 'The folks felt obliged to tell him about the dig last night when he showed up again. As you saw, he's not happy but he's family. He needed to know.'

'Of course. I appreciate that. But Australia is

home to some of the world's oldest fossils. Like Aboriginal art in hidden caves deep in the outback desert country, they're an equally priceless heritage.'

'I dig it.' She groaned at his pun but his lazy chuckle made her feel warm and safe. 'Don't worry, Darcy, we're on the same page,' he continued. When he laid a hand gently on her leg, heat from the touch surged right through her body. 'My Dad and I have been collecting on our land all our lives and saving anything we find. As you saw when you arrived in the homestead.'

She shrugged. 'Sadly, not everyone is of the same patriotic mind as us. Out here,' she gestured behind them toward the dig site, 'that heritage is mostly unprotected. There's no security guard on every fossil site so it's open to being stolen or lost or destroyed. It only takes a few greedy rogue collectors to muscle in and snatch it up.' She snapped her fingers for emphasis.

For the first time, Darcy noticed Mitch seemed uncomfortable as he scuffed his boot in the dirt and squinted out over the waterhole.

'Can't promise Hart will stay quiet. He likes an audience. And he's not attached to this property like the rest of the family. As you heard, he doesn't believe you should be out here. Fortunately that was Dad's decision backed by me so you can imagine there's plenty of tension in the homestead at the moment. Well, more than usual,' his full mouth tilted into a grin, 'now that Hart's home again.'

'That's a pity. I had hoped we could contain wider knowledge of our project as long as possible.' Darcy turned sideways to look directly into Mitch's disarming blue eyes. 'I'm not being dramatic here. I've done my research and had firsthand experience. There's a hunger for fossils and they fetch huge prices. They're traded across the globe. Locally, wealthy dealers can pay a fee to landowners and take what they like. It makes me sick.'

She shook her head. 'Fossils are precious and hard won. You've seen our enthusiastic underpaid band of diggers back there. But there's no specific fossil protection legislation in the country so it's damned impossible to stop the black market. If I can block even one operation then I'll try. Sorry.' Darcy pulled a grin, fully aware of Mitch's concentrated gaze on her the whole time. 'Getting carried away.'

'I have no problem with your passion.'

Darcy raised her eyebrows and hesitated, amused yet afraid to look across at the expression on his face. Was he being cheeky or not? He had a dry sense of humour, natural and unforced, that she was growing to love but sometimes she wasn't quite sure which way to take this man.

She went on. 'The struggle probably sounds

impossible and you're thinking why bother? We scientists would love more protection and commercial dealers want more freedom to make money. I know I'm biased for my own professional benefit but if there was some sort of penalty and deterrent, maybe people would have second thoughts.'

'The fossils are damned lucky to have you on their side.'

He was teasing. 'Couldn't help not be growing up close to my Grandpa Joe. He was always exploring and fossicking and we kids all tagged along. He passed on his enthusiasm and respect for Aboriginal culture carved into rock faces, made us aware of tools and relics hidden beneath the soil. Guess that's where my digging mania started. And my father's work and love of the outback too, I guess. Clearly inherited,' she laughed. 'Science seemed a logical choice for university.'

Her enthusiasm crushed soon after she qualified. But that was a story for another time.

'A few years back they found a fossil on a remote station site in the Territory near the West Australian border. It was on a riverbank that flooded every wet season and was highly eroded. It became critical to be recovered which proved tricky. Needed to be winched up a cliff.'

'Think I read about that.' Mitch frowned. 'What happened to it?'

'It's on display in Alice Springs. It's a

diprotodon, classed as megafauna, related to wombats but as big as a rhinoceros. Two metres tall and weighing about three tons.'

Mitch whistled softly. 'Impressive. Must go check it out one day. Get to visit your family much up there?'

How did they get from Hartley to her family, Darcy wondered? 'Sometimes.' Not enough, she knew. 'Christmas, everyone lands at the folks' place. Joe Junior usually cooks so it's all about the food and wallowing in the pool.'

'It's a great time for families to come together.'

'Yeah. Family is important,' she said softly, knowing her personal and professional recovery was due to their support but never having really considered settling down with one of her own. Preoccupied with her hunt, there hadn't been much time for deeper relationships these past years. So she had kept her rare romances light, easy to break.

Darcy knew if Grandpa Joe had been alive back then at the time of her trouble, he would have been horrified at his granddaughter's treatment. No doubt waving a banner of protest at the cause or, more likely, getting in there without any thought of danger to himself, right alongside her to help expose the criminals.

From an early age by association with him he had instilled in her and her siblings a strong sense of good and bad people, right and wrong, implanting a strong legacy of justice.

'How do you think this fossil find will affect your family? I'm sure the museum will be back for more digs,' Darcy asked when she eventually tugged herself back from thought, easy in her surroundings and Mitch's stirring company.

'You mean if it's substantial?' She nodded. 'Not much,' he admitted, grinning. 'The folks will stay on the station. Hart probably won't. I'll be between *Matilda Downs* and my own place. Life will continue pretty much as it has for generations. Outback's in our blood. The Beaumonts are meant to be out here but I'm sure Dad and I are of the same mind about allowing the museum future access to the fossil site, or any others they find on the property. Whatever unfolds for the station, permission to access that area will remain open.'

'Wow. That would be awesome.' But Darcy's attention had been diverted by his reference to *my place.* 'You have your own property, then?'

'Yep. An hour further west and then it turns north into the foothills of the jump up.'

'Sheep?'

'Yep. Might try cattle too and there are a few other ideas I'm kicking around on my mental blackboard. I guess your work can take you anywhere.'

'It's pretty much focused on Queensland for now. I'm based in Brisbane and this *is* dinosaur country but in the future I'll go wherever life takes me. I've got to tell you though, it's been exciting getting out of the city and back into the country even just for two weeks.'

'It's exciting having you out here,' he drawled.

Darcy flashed him a look of surprise over her shoulder. He didn't move at first but when he caught her eye, not correcting any possible misunderstanding in his comment, she was still left wondering if he meant her presence personally or sharing in the thrill of his fossil find. Bit of a tease if it was the former since Mitch Beaumont was all country boy and easy on the eye and there was no doubt about their interest in each other. A simmering magnetism had long ago kicked into life between them. Maybe her time out here in this beautiful place was the break she needed to figure out more about herself and her future. To date all her efforts so far were committed to her goal.

Mitch's query about what she planned next had left her thinking. She had been focused on walking a treadmill these past years. A body could waste a whole chunk of life by being too single-minded. Especially if it all came to nothing. Maybe she needed to reassess that. Yet Darcy also knew she would find it hard, if not impossible, to give up her purpose. Not after all this time when she sensed she was getting so close.

Realising how much time she had spent with

Mitch and losing track of everything else in the process as though they had both existed in their own bubble all the while, Darcy made the first move.

She rose to her feet where they had been sitting at the water's edge hugging their knees, chatting and sharing lives. She had enjoyed and appreciated these quiet moments with Mitch. She brushed off the seat of her jeans as he stood too and looked down at her. Eye to eye, both in boots, she could look straight into those magnetic blue eyes.

'Appreciate you understanding about Hart,' he murmured.

'Not much we can do about that except stay alert. You staying to help?' she probed. 'Probably morning tea already.'

He hesitated. 'Maybe later.'

'Sure.' Darcy smiled widely to hide her disappointment. Selfish and unrealistic because this guy was helping to run *Matilda Downs* and his own station as well. He'd have plenty to do elsewhere. 'I'll contact you when we can more completely uncover the bones and let you know exactly what we've identified.'

'Look forward to it.'

Cool as you like, he unzipped her windcheater. Darcy grew all hot and bothered at his sudden action, not objecting to his boldness but wondering where it was going. Maybe he intended sliding those strong tanned arms around her waist? Then she understood. His gaze lowered to her chest as he read today's t-shirt slogan *Sleep when you're extinct.*

He shook his head and grinned. 'Fair enough.' He half waved, ran a hand through his hair before he replaced his Akubra and walked away.

Darcy found herself standing awhile watching the floating dust of his departing ute and already anticipating his return. Whenever that might be. He hadn't said and seemed distracted by something. She sighed as she headed back to the dig site. Aren't we all?

She was puzzled when Mitch didn't return. But his brother did. Her whole body tensed when his ominous black vehicle quietly crept onto to the perimeter of the field site, pulled to a stop and just parked.

Darcy's alarm aerials immediately shot up and she cringed, knowing the diggers had worked hard for days with everyone focusing to help on the main and biggest fossil find. Its shape was revealing and growing in exposure. Even an amateur like Hartley would see that this dig relic was substantial. An uneasy instinct told her that he should be the last person to know.

He sat for a long time in his truck. On her hands and knees alongside the others with picks, rock hammers and brushes, Darcy kept him in her peripheral vision but she tried not to be too obvious in her furtive glances. He would know she was fully aware of his arrival and disturbing presence.

'Who's the visitor?' Helen murmured as they scratched away together.

Darcy snapped a quick glance over her shoulder, pretending disinterest. 'Um … Mitch's brother I think.'

'He has a camera.'

Darcy's hands stilled at her task. Shit. Go over and approach him or play wait and see? If he had already taken photos, she could hardly make a scene and try to confiscate his camera. The best she could do at some point was inform Mitch about his brother's dubious tactics.

Within moments, Hart left his truck and strolled closer. Darcy braced herself for another unpleasant encounter. With the man's poor personality and attitude, it was a no brainer.

She rose and brushed herself down, deliberately standing between Hart and their specimen to block his view and stop further evidence leaving the site. The damage was already done but she could at least try to lessen further fallout.

'Morning,' she called out pleasantly, climbing out of the depression created by their work. Nodding to the camera hanging around his neck, brazenly obvious, she said, 'Sorry, I'd prefer you not take photos. This is a museum site for now and there are dangers, as you can appreciate.' She stretched the truth.

'I appreciate nothing of what you're doing

here,' he said, unsmiling. 'I'm recording any possible destruction to the landscape.'

Yeah and pigs are flying as we speak. Darcy took a deep breath. 'I've lived in the outback all my life. I know this kind of country. Apart from that one big hole,' she gestured behind to their contained field site, 'which your brother dug up by the way,' she pointed out, 'it's an unpastured Mitchell grass paddock that we have a permit to explore.'

Darcy stared him down, frustrated, letting him know she was familiar with life out here. In the context of size, this excavation was barely even a postage stamp.

'What are you finding?' He tried looking around her but Darcy stubbornly moved as he did.

'Fossils.'

His gaze narrowed at her flippancy. 'Looks big.'

'It's a number of smaller remains.' Not entirely untrue but it was beginning to comprise one very exciting whole. 'But we'll keep working anyway. It may prove worthwhile but these digs aren't always successful.' She shrugged. 'Sometimes the small stuff can be revealing in its own way though.'

'I hear fossils are worth money?'

Snap! Darcy felt a small kick of triumph. Now she was getting somewhere. The fool was giving his own game away, revealing the true underlying reason for his sudden curiosity. Would Hartley even *need* the money? Life on the land could be hard but the Beaumonts seemed to be doing more than just making ends meet. Maybe for Mitch's brother it was more a case of simply wanting it.

'They're really only valuable to museums for research.' She moved away, trying to turn his back to the hollow and lead his attention elsewhere. 'Would you care to see the rest of our setup?' She had no intention of taking him anywhere near her research tent though where she kept the smaller labelled fossil pieces. In the light of this irregular visit, she must rethink their safe keeping.

'Nice try,' he grunted.

He persisted with more questions all aimed at extracting information more suitable to commercial interests. Throughout the uncomfortable conversation, Darcy made every attempt to casually minimise the importance of their discovery. But with every squint of Hartley's brow and grilling enquiry, her mind ticked over.

For a man who, according to his brother, never had any interest in fossils before, it was impossible to ignore the theory that niggled at the back of her mind. Darcy believed Hartley's fixation was not generated solely on his own account. The moment he had mentioned money, the puzzle pieces slowly sorted themselves out until her intuition put them together and clicked them into place.

Hartley Beaumont could be working alone but more likely it was for someone else and Darcy's heart dropped at the sickening possibility of who exactly that might be. The bastard would never dare show his face but it didn't matter because it was now obvious he was already working against her behind the scenes. This intolerable man standing before her would have been promised a cut. She knew from asking questions that pay offs could be staggering.

Well, family or not, Mitch and his parents had to be informed of this complication and its consequences. Which were serious and meant she would need to disclose her past to put the whole situation into perspective. Daunting thought but with today's developments, it was approaching time for the truth all around. About Hartley and about herself.

Darcy moved in a daze like a zombie, playing tolerant host and dogging Hartley's side, not letting him out of her sight and with every footstep silently begging him to leave. Eventually, and way overdue, he did. Darcy made no attempt to hide her relief as he graced her with a smug grin and friendly wave driving away in his big black shiny truck.

Darcy kept her arms folded across her chest and did not acknowledge his departure in any way. She had turned her back on him long before he left. She was too busy thinking ahead about her whole professional world on the brink of being thrown into chaos again. Her mind raced as to how best she would protect her buried treasure and team while tracking her hovering enemy.

But her fears were also laced with a rising excitement at the possibility of success in what had been a lonely five year endeavour.

Chapter 5

With Ed and Nina in Longreach for a few days investigating future options for *Matilda Downs* that would be fair for everyone, Mitch felt obliged to stay close to the homestead.

It was a sad state of affairs when you couldn't even trust your own brother but he was nowhere to be seen when he drove up to the front gate after his chat to Darcy at the waterhole. Only the dogs came to greet him and Hartley's truck was gone from the cottage.

It didn't take much for Mitch's thoughts to drift back to Darcy. He wondered what she would think if she knew he would love to steal her away for a few hours and take her out to his place. Because she was a country woman he wanted to share his small corner of the world with her. He knew she would appreciate his outback space. He would sound her out and see if it could be worked in while she was around.

He knew he had delayed her from returning to the dig this morning. As he had left and checked out her t-shirt – a fast move, he acknowledged, and one for which he made no apologies, nor did she object – the lights in her dark hair and that soft mouth so close had driven a need to taste the lips that took a truck load of control to resist. He knew it would be damn good to feel that woman in his arms.

He demolished a ploughman's sandwich for lunch washed down with a mug of tea then headed out on another lambing run.

When he returned, Hart's truck was still missing but an unfamiliar four wheel drive was parked in front of the homestead. He knew every district vehicle and this wasn't one of them.

Mitch drew up alongside, noting the rental sticker and climbed the steps to the front veranda where a middle aged man rose from one of the cane chairs to greet him. Tall, dark hair boasting a few strands of grey distinguished looking. Someone half important? He took in the neat pressed trousers and crisp shirt. City bloke. Outback wannabe? Mitch knew he was being cynical but with Darcy's revelation of worrying events on the dig and Hart's frustrating return, he was running low on tolerance.

'I hope you're not selling insurance,' Mitch quipped to see how he reacted and handled himself.

'Mr. Beaumont.'

The guy knew him? Not totally unusual. The

family had been in the district for generations. All the same, Mitch wasn't comfortable starting out at a disadvantage. Out here was his territory and he preferred to be on top of things.

For some reason the visitor's practised smile annoyed the hell out of him. And he hated being formally addressed. Everyone hereabouts used Christian or nick names.

'And you are?' Mitch asked as they shook hands.

'Marshall Stirling.'

Announced with a degree of pride and Mitch conceded it did sound impressive. Judging by the man's bearing, it was meant to be. He didn't want to be unfair so he reserved his first impression but he usually took a fair stock of a character up front. So far, this guy didn't measure up.

'How can I help you?' Mitch offered, indicating the veranda chairs behind them, not intending to invite the man indoors.

Stirling's gaze scanned the grassland spinifex. 'Inspiring landscape.'

The man's procrastination with forced pleasantries set Mitch's radar humming. 'Our family loves it. What brings you out here?' he cut to the chase.

When he still wasn't forthcoming, the man's pause reduced the length of Mitch's patience, already thin, even further. It suggested a reluctance for some reason and a man had to wonder why.

'This is dinosaur country,' Stirling said eventually.

Ah, now they were getting somewhere. That narrowed possibilities but also raised questions. 'Certainly is.'

'I'm a Professor of Paleontology. I hear you have a find.'

Mitch's instinct was to be suspicious but only because Darcy had expressed concerns. She didn't strike him as being alarmist so he trusted her logic. This guy likely heard the news from the science community but his announcement was pompous. He would play his cards close. His gut feeling was still kicking around and he had learned to listen to it.

'My father and I have been finding bits and pieces on our property for decades. Nothing new. Like plenty of others hereabouts. Word has obviously spread though,' he pulled a tight grin.

'Dinosaurs are a specialised field of science.'

'You obviously all communicate well then.'

'I'd be interested to take a look.'

The outback levelled people. Despite his eminence in title and profession at least, this guy didn't fit. Odd. Knowing he was going bush you'd think he would have dressed for a dig like Darcy and her crew. Mitch saw this performer being more at home behind a desk.

'Might be possible. Need to check with the team leader.'

'I know Darcy Manning,' he said with smooth confidence.

The news didn't surprise Mitch at all. Plot just kept getting thicker. His guest not only knew about the fossil find and location but that a dig was underway and the people involved. Course it could have just taken a phone call to the museum but somehow Mitch doubted that. The locals would be cagey until the dig results were fully known and disclosed.

'Then she'll be pleased to see you,' he said wryly, suspecting otherwise. 'Where did you meet?'

'Up in the Territory. Know much about her?'

The guy was fishing and it didn't sound promising. 'Enough. She came recommended by the museum.'

'Don't be fooled. She has a history.'

Mitch resented the guy's dismissive tone. 'Really? In what way?'

'Legal misdemeanour early in her career. Got too big too soon. Woman trying to make it big in a man's world.'

Mitch felt offence on Darcy's behalf. From his first meeting with her he had seen nothing but an adventurous Territory girl, sexy beyond belief, passionate about her work. Yet here was a fellow colleague casting doubt on her character. He found it hard to equate this guy's version of Darcy with the woman he knew himself. Male ego on Stirling's behalf? Didn't appreciate a little professional competition?

'Interesting. And yet the museum employed her,' Mitch said.

'Maybe they weren't aware of all the facts.'

'Surprised to hear it. You said yourself paleontology is a small circle,' Mitch challenged.

'She's a competitive female.'

'Didn't know ambition was a crime.'

Mitch wouldn't have used that word around Darcy. Driven maybe but he doubted she would tread on people to advance her career. By contrast, he sensed this Professor just might. Mitch let the mess in his gut slide for now until he had more facts.

'Thanks for the heads up anyway.' Mitch fished for his mobile. 'I'll make a call.'

Ironically, as he stepped down from the veranda and walked away out of earshot, his phone rang.

Somehow, in the wake of Hartley's appearance on site, Darcy managed to carry on but her concentration was shot to pieces for the day. She knew she should phone Mitch but that call would mean opening up about everything in her past so she delayed. Besides, she would rather do that conversation in person. Maybe he would come out later.

Instead, mid-afternoon at tea break, Darcy checked her sat phone on its solar charger back at her tent. Because it was nagging her, she decided to brave the call and moved away from the trees into open space to have a direct line of sight between her phone and the sky. After a moment's hesitation, she pressed Mitch's number.

He answered immediately. No backing out now, she sighed, taking a deep breath.

'This is a coincidence,' he replied. 'I was about to call you.'

'Oh.' He had been thinking of her? 'I know you're busy on the station but I'd like a chance to talk with you. I need to tell you something.'

'Can it wait? There's someone here at the homestead to see you.'

Darcy's mind raced. 'Who?'

'A Professor Stirling.'

Her heart almost stopped beating and her throat went dry. This wasn't happening! The nightmare was starting up all over again. Her entire body chilled with dread. Her old enemy had dared present himself. Brazen move. To intimidate, of course. And so soon.

Well, she took herself under control. She was ready for this. 'He's...um an old colleague from the Territory,' Darcy replied warily.

'So he said.'

'He did?'

'You don't sound pleased about his arrival.'

'Let's just say he's no friend.'

'Will I bring him out?'

'Yeah. Why not.'

As she paced her campsite and awaited their arrival, Darcy knew that with his professional eye, Stirling would immediately see exactly what they had found. If it was anyone else in the science world, she wouldn't mind. In fact, she would be excited to talk shop but this monster would use it to his own advantage.

Not surprising he made it a priority to find out where she was working. Even more interesting that he should travel all the way out here himself. He must know the fossil was considerable or he wouldn't have bothered. But apart from herself, only the Beaumont family, the museum staff back in Brisbane and the field crew out here on site knew that.

Darcy dared not reflect on exactly who had leaked but they may not know this man was treacherous. And she herself would never be free of him until she could prove his guilt. So far he had been too smart to let that happen but she was closing in and ready for another battle. With each confrontation she hoped it was her last.

Now she not only had to face Stirling again but she hadn't told Mitch about Hartley's weird behaviour and there was still another revealing conversation to take place between them about her past. Trouble was, she wanted Mitch to know her side, the truth. Her deepest fear was that the Professor may have already dropped hints and planted doubts in Mitch's mind about her. He was a master at distorting facts.

Darcy impatiently squinted north back toward the track leading from the homestead out here to the waterhole and nearby dig site. When the tell-tale dust cloud approached, she stood astride, hands on hips, primed for this unwelcome reunion.

She had no intention of taking Stirling across to the workings. Bad enough he knew the location but he would ask and out of professional courtesy, she must oblige. The thought made her wretched with simmering fury.

As her adversary stepped from Mitch's dusty ute, Darcy thought the sleazy scum bag could wipe that smug grin off his face or she would do it for him. Pretending like nothing untoward had ever happened between them before.

'Professor.' Darcy nodded to show she would not be intimidated. 'Surprised to see you out here. Visiting all the current digs in the country to assess their worth?'

Her blatant slur was not lost on him. His cold eyes glittered with contemptuous anger but his lips spread into the fake cheesy smile for which he was renowned. She ought to know. He had flashed it enough for the cameras and newspapers all those years ago in Darwin. Back then, she had been charmed, daunted and finally fooled, but not today.

'Darcy. Nice to meet you again, too,' he ground out with forced civility.

He was furious and she was stoked. She also noted he didn't give her the respect of calling her Doctor. Keeping that in mind she kept her cool and determined to convey as little as possible.

'Always professionally interested in new finds.'

'You mean personally, don't you?'

His narrow gaze sliced through her and he said low, 'Be careful, Darcy.'

She glared at him. 'Around you, Professor, always.' From the corner of her eye, Darcy noticed a hovering Mitch take a step closer. 'And for your information it's Doctor now, thank you. But I'm sure you knew that as you know everything else about me.'

They glowered at each other. She could handle this man and, given half a chance if the opportunity rose, would bring him down. This unworthy piece of shit thought he was God's gift to science but one day his time would come.

'Not in a private plane today?' she quipped, glancing over Mitch's shoulder. The country's boy's lazy gaze told her he wasn't missing a thing but she would have a lot of explaining to do later.

In the wake of her forthright outburst, Darcy was thrilled to see Stirling emotionally stumbling and off balance. Amazing what only a few more years' knowledge could do for a person's self-confidence. But he still outranked her and that made Darcy sick to her stomach so she forced herself to behave and try to be polite. She sighed. She had better upgrade her manners.

'If you have any questions I'm happy to oblige.'

'Just one.'

And she knew what that would be. Darcy raised her eyebrows, remaining silent.

'Where's this fossil?'

Darcy didn't respond but turned her back and slowly led the way. Over her shoulder she said to Mitch, 'You coming, too?'

'If you like.'

She nodded.

Mitch kept his distance. Impossible not to notice the stiffness in Darcy's movements as she wandered with the Professor, not too close to the dig's outer boundaries.

Too obvious that she had been reluctant to see this man or show him the busy dig. The band of volunteers all laboriously kneeling down, hunched over and beavering away at its edges, brushed and scraped over and round the perimeter of their emerging fossil find, revealing too much to this man Darcy clearly disliked.

As Mitch leaned back against one of the supply utes, he unashamedly watched Darcy from concern as well as healthy male pleasure and appreciation. She was giving nothing. Stood arms folded, saying little. Pretty much a one-way conversation. Must have been something serious to bring out this uptight woman he hadn't seen before.

Judging by his short growling comments, the Professor seemed frustrated. Darcy's intention he was sure, and withheld a grin. Which left him intrigued and not a little concerned about the origins behind this tense encounter. This steely side of the softer humorous woman he thought he knew was a stunning contrast in personalities.

Darcy didn't concede an inch during the visit. The Professor strutted about importantly but from the firm set of her mouth and strained body language, she remained stubbornly rebellious. She didn't weaken. Kept up the charade the whole time and he admired her spirit, plainly begrudging every moment she was forced to spend with the guy. He wasn't a gambling man but he would bet she damned well needed a break from him. Like now. She was wound up tighter than he had seen any human being in a long while.

He pushed himself away from the supply ute and ambled toward them. Darcy turned at his approach, spreading a warm knowing glance of gratitude for the interruption.

'Hate to interrupt,' he lied, 'but the folks are away and I'd rather not leave the homestead unattended too long. Be obliged if we could head back soon,' he said easily to Stirling who scowled with aggravation.

'Yes, I'm sure the Professor is eager to get back to more comfortable surroundings and I need to get back to work,' Darcy said bluntly.

She snapped a curt smile, then spun on her boot heels and turned her back to head down to join the volunteers in the hollowed ground, leaving Mitch to stroll with a bristling Stirling back to his ute parked at Darcy's campsite.

Darcy felt bad about her careless attitude in dismissing Mitch. She didn't give a fig for the Professor but Mitch's opinion mattered and she would need to reveal her reasons. She only hoped he accepted her explanation and apology, and understood.

Her thoughts raged. She injected the energy from her anger at Stirling's arrogant appearance into her labours as she worked alongside the team.

Helen eyed her strangely when she rejoined them. 'Another interloper?' Darcy nodded. 'You know him?'

'He looks harmless enough,' she muttered in reply, 'but he's trouble.'

'We're all on watch,' Helen said softly in reassurance. 'We have this guy's back.' She nodded down to the fossil being gradually exposed to the world again.

Touched, Darcy continued, feeling better after hearing Helen's supportive words. She pressed on with the task of mixing plaster in her bucket to continue covering the top surface of the precious fossil with its protective field jacket before being carefully turned over and doing the same to the bottom half. A few crumbling edge pieces had been reinforced with special glue to help stabilise and keep them together.

When she reflected on the significance of what she and her team had precisely excavated to isolate it, a renewed frustration built up inside her at Stirling's audacity. He now knew its vast significance and what this discovery was truly worth. She had seen his gleaming predatory gaze sharpen which set her on edge.

Should anyone wish to try, it would be difficult removing the fossil where it lay not only because of its size and their activated night patrols but also because the field site was so close to the camp. Any intruders would be immediately detected. She must warn the men on guard to be extra vigilant. Still, it rankled that Stirling might find a way.

But at some point in its setting, removal or transfer to the lab, he would try. The implications terrified her. That the result of all this daily physical effort was now in genuine danger. Adding extra tension she could do without right now. Worse, when she explained her past to Mitch and connection with Stirling, it would place their warm budding friendship in jeopardy.

Her depth of attraction and hunger for the charismatic outback man had hit her without warning from their first meeting at the homestead. She ached inside that it could all be lost before being given a chance to even start. She sensed genuine returning vibes from Mitch. Not normally given to the slightest response to men until her current life's purpose was achieved, Darcy felt a cruel fear of deprivation that the powerful draw she felt toward Mitch might end.

She hadn't dared to allow herself any deeper feelings in the past but Mitch Beaumont mattered. His cheeky smile could light up a whole town but there were some tricky bridges to cross before she let herself have any hopes in his direction. Right about now, with all the obstacles that lay ahead, she would clutch at the smallest signal of promise sent her way to get her through the forthcoming ordeal.

She was under no illusion that her final challenge would be easy now Stirling had surfaced again – in person no less. The game was on. His familiar pattern was emerging and her life once more would be disrupted.

But this was it. No more. Time to put herself out there in a big way. If she came to any harm in the process, so be it. But hopefully the danger will not have been in vain.

Hardly able to enjoy a mouthful of yet another one of Dawnie's superb evening meals through worry, Darcy made a final circuit in the evening twilight around the field site and her work tent with a brief word to Murray, the first on duty for the night.

She retreated to her own camp, envious of the crew all seated around the main campfire, their laughter carrying to her across the stillness of the late winter night. Close by her tent she heard splashing as birds settled down around the waterhole and sparks rose like fireflies as she poked her fire pit logs into life to help set the billy sing to a boil.

After a while, immense relief curled through her when she saw headlights advancing. Nerves churned her insides as the vehicle stopped under the trees and Mitch's familiar outline turned from a shadowed image to the real thing up close.

No big hat tonight. He ran a hand through his sandy waves.

'Hey,' she murmured, rising from the opposite side of the fire to where he now stood.

'He's gone,' was all he said and all she needed to know.

Her shoulders drooped with relief. 'Billy's boiled,' she said awkwardly. 'Feel like a cuppa?' Unsure beneath the steady gaze he sent across the fire, she indicated behind to the esky alongside her tent. 'Or I have a beer if you prefer.'

'Hot drink will be fine.'

He sauntered around the fire, disturbingly closer, watching as she made his tea, adding milk and sugars, remembering the way he liked it. When she handed it across to him, of course their fingers were destined to touch in the process and heat flared between them.

'We can sit on the ground or I have camp chairs.'

'Dirt is fine,' he drawled.

They settled together, stretching out their long legs toward the fire's warmth.

'Pleased you came out.' Darcy decided to jump right into it.

'To be honest, I'm finding it hard to keep away.'

She thrilled to hear it and hugged his words to her heart. 'Wasn't sure you would return after my abrupt goodbye,' she admitted. 'Sorry to be a bit gruff.'

'You had your reasons.'

'And I'm pleased to see the back of him.' She paused. 'I had another visitor this morning, too. Equally worrying. Hartley.'

Mitch snapped her a quick scowl. 'Strange. He hasn't been back to the homestead since yesterday. I didn't notice his truck. He must have deliberately cut across the paddock from the property road.'

'Didn't want to be seen?' Darcy ventured carefully. 'Because his visit was also less than pleasant. He sat in his vehicle for a while. Helen noticed he was taking photos and eventually strolled over with a decent looking camera slung about his neck. Made no effort to hide it.'

'Never knew he had one. Seems there's a lot I don't know about my big brother,' Mitch murmured. 'We've never been close,' he admitted with a note of regret.

'He said he was filming evidence of landscape destruction but based on the fact you said he has never shown interest in fossils before,' Darcy hesitated before adding, 'I believe he might be taking them for someone else.'

Mitch frowned, staring into the fire and softly cursed. 'Sounding suspicious.'

'Unfortunately I have to agree. I'm sorry Mitch but it's too much of a coincidence. Hartley films the dig site this morning and within hours what do you know? My favourite Professor shows up.'

'You reckon there's a connection? But how would Hart have known who to contact?'

Darcy scoffed. 'Trust me on this. I know from personal experience that Professor Marshall Stirling would go to no end of trouble to find a dollar in a dark room. For him, I've discovered, money talks. Stirling would have found a way. Infiltrated the locals. Spread the word. His methods don't have limits. He only befriends people who are useful to him.

'You saw the way he was dressed today. Certainly not for hard work on a dig. I've seen his gated private residence in Darwin. Think elite enclaves and water views. Plus he owns a damned nice motor yacht that he moors in Cullen Bay marina. And all on a paleo's salary?' She scoffed. 'Professors teach. Not huge bucks.'

'How do you know all this?'

'I've made it my business. For the sake of my health.'

'So,' Mitch prompted softly, 'what's your history with this guy?'

'Extremely unpleasant.'

Chapter 6

'I'm listening,' Mitch said. Probably because she hesitated and didn't immediately respond, he added, 'Because you're a female?'

'Hell no,' Darcy chuckled. 'Our contact went way beyond that.' She drew up her knees and wrapped her arms around them. 'It started at university. Now of course I wish I'd never met him but back then, before I knew better, he was a senior peer. Someone to look up to. Before I caught on. Others chose to play dumb but they knew.'

Her voice lowered with distaste. 'My problem was I couldn't let it go and decided to do something about it. Privately. Discovered it way too risky asking any other colleagues. Stirling's an influential man. Turned out I was betrayed anyway.'

Mitch didn't say a word but shuffled cosily closer so their knees and shoulders touched. She grinned to herself. He might want more distance after he heard what she had to say.

'After that fossil find in the Territory a few years back, other discoveries were claimed but oddly enough no digs eventuated and any possible pieces mysteriously never materialised or made it into any museum so everyone thought it was just rumours. As far as I know, no one ever followed it up. That's when I first grew seriously suspicious. I checked out the news leads, discovered substance to the story but that further information had been suppressed. That's when I made my biggest mistake, got excited and stupidly raised the irregularity with the Professor. Of course he told me to forget it. I thought it strange that he didn't show any interest or sign of concern to at least investigate the reports.'

'What did you do?'

'Got sneaky. Watched and took photos of whoever Stirling met with and I can tell you there were plenty of encounters in lonely places. I soon learnt how to stay out of sight. But it grew frustrating when I couldn't nail him down to anything specific. Seemed he organised everything himself but never got his own hands dirty. Always managed to keep at arm's length. So I started taking more risks.'

'Why am I not surprised?' Mitch murmured.

Her stomach curled with heat at the affection in his voice. 'I did some research that allowed me to get closer, gave me access to his staff and his office.'

'You didn't!' he drawled.

'Didn't what?' she countered, turning to face him, an action that brought them breathtakingly close. If she leaned in just a little closer…

'Get caught.'

Darcy looked away again toward the fire, now glowing coals, and cleared her throat. 'Not for a while,' she swiftly defended her actions. 'I was greener then and eager. I let my purpose cloud caution. And I…um…did one or two devious things that pushed boundaries.'

'Am I game to ask?'

Darcy grew decidedly uncomfortable because her misdemeanours had been culpable. And she must reveal a side to her that she wasn't sure she wanted Mitch to know. But she must.

'Looking back I'm not proud of crossing the line but I knew in my gut even back then and despite being foolishly naïve that Stirling was crooked. I hated that a distinguished man in a suit who tossed blackmail and threats about with abandon, thought he was above the law and could get away with the theft of fossil treasures.' With rising irritation, she admitted, 'I just hadn't been able to dig deep enough to link him with his higher connections or the actual crimes. It's a carefully protected system and I still haven't cracked it. I'm missing something,' she scowled. 'How the fossils actually leave the country. Where the handovers take place.'

'Shouldn't you leave this to the law?'

'I have some evidence but not enough to convict him. I only need one link in the smugglers' chain to make a wrong move and we might have something to work with.'

'So how did the Professor find you out?'

Darcy pushed out a heavy sigh of exasperation. 'In the end it was a piece of paper and another woman.' Maybe if she said this quick it wouldn't sound so bad. 'I infiltrated the Professor's office after hours and went through his files.'

'You burgled?'

Trying to sound innocent and offended, she said, 'I just photographed a few things that seemed possible leads. Downloaded emails onto a USB, that kind of thing. And at a party,' despite her dire situation at the time, Darcy smiled to herself in memory, 'I flirted with one of Stirling's associates. Made advances, draped myself all over him. He was single and he was eyeing me off so I tried flattery and pumped him for information.'

She wasn't particularly proud of using feminine wiles to get what she wanted. It wasn't in character for the Darcy that went bush with Grandpa Joe but it *was* the woman who'd been raised to know right from wrong.

She waited for any sign of revulsion from Mitch. Instead he just gave a low lazy laugh. 'Darcy Manning you are one wicked woman. Did it work?'

'Might have if an ex-girlfriend hadn't appeared and grown jealous. She made a scene and hurled abuse and glasses. Next day I was called into Stirling's office and questioned. I thought I explained innocently enough and apologised for my over indulgence in alcohol – faked by the way – and my poor behaviour causing trouble but the Professor's radar had already locked onto me. He pressured me to behave or I would be fired. I'd come so close but I grew so angry at the injustice of it all, in my foolish youthful exuberance, I played my hand. Took all my so-called evidence to the museum and the police knowing the proof was flimsy.

'My claims were investigated but Stirling's big shot lawyers on a juicy payroll accused and implicated *me* instead. Boy were those suits smooth and did they twist the evidence. Turned the spotlight away from their culprit client and questioned me about my agenda. Used just enough doubt to swing a decision their way. I was labelled a career climber and a troublemaker. He set out to publicly and legally shame me and he won. Technically, the university was my place of work and I had access. It wasn't a break in but to avoid a scandal and prison, my lawyer made a deal for fines with an agreement that I should voluntarily resign. Which, of course, cost me my reputation and career. For a very long while.'

Mitch reached out for her hand and squeezed

it. 'Sorry you went through that.'

God after all she'd just admitted, he still liked her? And he was twining their fingers together? Darcy began to grasp at a tiny ray of hope that there just might be someone else passionate about fossils too who might stand alongside her and believe her in all this.

'The Professor was cleared but my name was mud. For a long time I did whatever menial work I could. I existed on my dignity and hard work. I clawed my way back, proved myself trustworthy and genuinely passionate about my scientific field. Paleontology is a cool career but far from cosy. After two years and with a supporting legal letter from my lawyer and some serious talking on my own behalf, I landed a full time job with a museum. Fossils are hot property right now and Stirling is exploiting it. I'm back in the game and on his trail again.'

'Are you sure this guy is guilty?'

'Absolutely. I believe this involves a major international crime ring. Stirling's time will come, and soon. There was no truth in any of their twisted slander,' Darcy flared indignantly. 'He almost succeeded in ruining me but I fought back. They tried to discredit me and shut me up but they failed. I'm still around and I intend to finish what I started.'

'You're a strong woman.' He hesitated. 'Is it all worth it?'

'Okay, you haven't known me long but I'm

prepared to stake my life on my instinct and my reputation. Tarnished though it may have been at one time. Every now and then you need to raise a little dust.' Mitch chuckled. ' Hell you've seen the Professor. What do you think?'

'If I was a cop I'd be tempted to check him out. And his disrespect toward you is revealing for such a smooth operator who dresses to impress. I'd say you have him worried.'

'Damned right,' Darcy retorted, 'and he has good reason.'

She put a brake on her resentment and backed off. Mitch had seemed impartial and understanding as he listened to her explanations. Far more than she probably deserved, remembering the trauma of the hurtful publicity and court case at the time. But who knew what opinion lay deeper in his mind? He sounded supportive enough but she *had* pushed legal boundaries.

'So the guy's probably a crim and others know it but no one is doing anything about it?'

'Except me. Ever since I challenged him I'm in his sights. He has no idea how much information I've gathered on him over the years.' Darcy grinned. 'And it's all safely under lock and key. Just in case he challenges me again.'

'You think he's that desperate?'

She nodded. 'Except I don't have that one final little piece of proof or testimony to clinch it.

So far no one is willing to stand up in court and back me up. It only needs one other person with the courage to speak out against him. But everyone's afraid. Understandably, people aren't prepared to risk everything. The Professor is into fossil smuggling deep but I'm convinced there's someone else even higher up. It wouldn't surprise me at all if it's worse than greedy black marketeers. Stirling likes the luxury lifestyle and is clearly their source but its organised crime that has the power and the money.'

Mitch whistled softly.

'They're untouchable and they're protecting the Professor. I just can't get close enough to catch them in the act and be implicated.'

Weary from a trying day stretching her brain and confiding her less than wholesome past, Darcy combed fingers through her tangled hair and stretched. And caught Mitch watching her with way more than simple admiration. Which blew her away because after her revelations she figured he had every reason to up and leave. Especially since she had no evidence of her claims. Yet. It was only her word against the world but she *would* see Stirling convicted no matter how long it took.

'I figure a woman like you will find a way.'

So she was enticed to brace the leading question on her mind. Mitch was an agreeable guy but he wouldn't dodge the truth. She would expect nothing less from him even though she might not like it.

'What kind of person do you think I am?'

She almost didn't want to know the answer but this country boy was eating into her heart. Growing important. It was vital he accept her for who she was now not what she had done, and look beyond her past. His respect and opinion was crucial. As an outsider even more than family.

'You mean your vibes?' Darcy shrugged and waited. 'For starters you're resisting me.'

'I am not!'

'Don't argue,' he chuckled softly, challenging her instinctive response. Now that it came down to it, daring her to openly acknowledge the growing truth between them. 'You absolutely love your work. A woman who actually enjoys getting dirty.'

'A little mud never hurt anybody.'

'The tomboy who turned into a scientist?'

'Maybe.'

Mitch's tone lowered to a murmur. 'You're a very beautiful woman, Darcy. Inside and out. You don't need make up and you don't use it. You tuck your hair under that cap but little strands escape. When you're working I'll bet you don't even feel them tickling your cheek.'

He didn't look at her but she felt every word he said with emotions that reached deep inside her. 'Don't sound so smug just because you're right.'

'And when you let down that hair, I just want to push my hands up into it and drag you close.'

Darcy gasped, stunned. His insinuation robbed her of breath. Wow, this man was giving her way more than she asked for. 'You're making me lose my mind, Beaumont.'

'So it's working then?'

'Wasn't fishing for compliments.'

'I know but everyone deserves a few now and then.'

In the dark, mint-scented gum leaves rustled just enough to cause shadows across the camp. Moonlight gleamed over the water on this clear starry outback night but something more than evening magic stirred around them.

Darcy guessed this man would know how to take a woman to heaven and back. A hard working country boy with a gentle side who had just opened up his heart, making her feel like a woman he wanted. Which made her feel vulnerable. She was just deciding to back off, needing more time to digest his complimentary opinion, when he made his move.

He stood up in front of her and held out his hands. Remembering to breathe, wary yet excited, she took them and he easily drew her up against him. With only dying firelight and a half moon, time stopped and they existed in an expectant shadowed cocoon. The air around them hummed with the pull of sensual heat.

Standing shoulder to boots, hands still linked,

noses and lips a breath away from each other, Darcy burned with need. God she wanted him. Why was he waiting? He'd just blown her mind with beautiful words any woman longed to hear from the man on the way to stealing her heart.

'You know I like you.' Hard for her to admit and even harder to voice. It had been a long time since she had trusted another man so much. 'Don't make me beg,' she whispered. 'Are you gonna kiss me or not?'

His hand touched her chin and his mouth captured hers. She closed her eyes, heart pounding and sank against him. At last, it felt so good to be lost in the right direction. No other man had ever hauled such strong feelings from the deepest part of her.

His strong arms embraced her with a fierce possession, letting her know she was his. While his kiss sent fireworks through her body, her hands stole over his shirt, edging their way inside at the collar and up around his neck.

Although her heart lifted with promise and a breathtaking temptation for this dreamy country man, the dynamics of an attraction in the midst of a major fossil dig and trying to nail Stirling to break a smuggling operation sent her mind reeling.

Their kiss deepened, mouths lingered, tasting and teasing. Darcy moaned softly when Mitch finally, reluctantly judging by his heavy sigh, pulled away.

'You are one tempting woman, Darcy Manning,' he drawled. 'To be continued?'

She knew what he was saying. As much as they wanted everything from each other and she ached at the thought of his naked skin against hers, it was the right man, wrong time. No need to rush. When it happened for the best reason it was gonna be so worth it. And the lips he pressed to her forehead just before he left were sweeter than kisses.

That night Darcy slept edgy and restless, not only from being kissed by a sexy outback man who now caused a rush in her heart each time she saw him. But after chatting to Mitch about the Professor, her mind was on high alert again flooded with thoughts of her life in upheaval back then and the ensuing emotional devastation that had ripped her self-confidence apart. Not to mention the unfairness of it all. She had struggled but she would never give up. All the same, she kept imagining noises in the night. Rustling, movement.

In the morning, still tousled and slow from lack of sleep, she unzipped her tent flap and emerged out into the pristine early morning sunlight. Her senses flared at the inviting aroma of Dawnie's coffee wafting across from the camp kitchen.

When she rubbed her eyes and performed a few yoga stretches to wake and loosen up, her gaze clear enough to truly take in the details of her surroundings, she froze and cursed. She sauntered slowly toward her classy motorbike, racy black with lots of silver, sitting way too low to the ground. Both bloody tyres were flat.

She dropped to her haunches and ran her hands and eyes over them. Slashed. Bastards. They were beyond fixing. She would need replacements. Private rage roared up inside her that someone had crept into camp, skulking with the cover of darkness and targeted her prized possession. Clearly none of the guys on night patrol had heard or seen anything or they would have woken her. Besides, their focus was on the fossil site and its protection. But she would check with them at breakfast.

So, who knew and appreciated a road machine like this? Who would understand the sting it caused to an owner when it was damaged? The answer came in a heartbeat. More than a coincidence with the Professor's arrival yesterday. He wouldn't stoop so low as to do anything this menial himself. Someone else was acting under his orders. And in turn he was probably taking orders himself from another person higher up.

Fast work, she acknowledged, feeling sick and furious. The intimidation had begun. Darcy sank onto the ground for a moment breathing deep to calm down.

A short time later when she had gathered

herself together, Darcy wandered firstly over to the central camp fire where some of her fellow workers were gathered, standing or seated in deck chairs and on logs close to the open fire, sipping morning cuppas. With everyone dog tired from the physical outdoor work all day, all declared they had slept soundly and not heard a thing. Including the guys who had shared the night patrol.

Darcy decided it best not to say anything and voice her growing concerns because she alone – at least for now - was clearly the target and while fossil *Mitch* was still in the ground anchored in soil and being protected day and night, he was safe.

After another of Dawnie's substantial breakfasts, Darcy moved away from the dig team nearer her work tent but out in the open so she had phone reception and called *Matilda Downs* homestead.

When Nina Beaumont answered, Darcy said with a brightness she certainly wasn't feeling. 'Hi Nina. You're back from Winton?'

'Yes, dear. It was a wonderful break. Lots sorted. How can I help you?'

Darcy picked up on Nina's brief reference to their family issues and prompt change of subject, alerted to do the same. 'I have a slight hitch I need to deal with. I presume you have a mechanic on the station?'

'We certainly do. Mack Harris. What's the

problem?'

'Two flat motorbike tyres.'

After a slight pause, Nina said, 'Really? That sounds strange.'

Darcy heard the concern in her voice. 'Certainly does. Considering I haven't ridden it for days. I'd call it suspicious actually.'

'Oh dear, Darcy. I'm sorry to hear that. Want me to phone the police station in town and get them to come out and take a look around?'

Darcy privately sighed. 'It's complicated, Nina. I'll explain another time, okay?'

'Of course, dear. You'll know best.'

'I'm not riding much and needing my bike at the moment anyway. It's just a damned inconvenience. Sorry.' She winced at her curse.

Darcy heard the smile in Nina's voice. 'Oh my goodness that's nothing, as you would know. We've both been around outback men all our lives. I've been exposed to blue language since I was a girl,' she chuckled.

Darcy gave her the tyre specifications.

Nina hesitated and said, 'We probably won't have those in stock here on the station. Might need to order them in from the garage in Winton.'

'Will that take long?'

'They can order in parts for overnight delivery. Meanwhile we could lend you Kit's bike in the machinery shed. It's only gathering dust under a tarpaulin while he's away.'

'Thanks. I'll let you know.'

'I'll send Mack out when he gets back later today and he can bring your bike back to the workshop in the ute. As soon as the tyres arrive he'll fit them and deliver it back.'

Darcy thanked her and ended the call. So when a familiar cloud of dust hailed his arrival within the hour she glanced up in surprise from her work table labelling a bunch of small fossil specimens the team had discovered yesterday. Mack must have finished early.

Darcy looked twice when she realised it wasn't the mechanic but a far more familiar visitor. The unexpected sight of him set a fluttering in her chest. Most undignified for a country girl trying to avoid men during this troubling time in her life. But Mitch Beaumont was turning into a problem, making her feel safe and happy.

As his ute pulled up and his beautiful border collie leapt from the back, he strolled toward her like he had all the time in the world, the dog excitedly dashing around their legs.

The man's eyes were still the same blue as any outback sky. She found it difficult to focus on the business at hand remembering his dynamite kiss last night, especially when he flashed his trademark wickedly sexy smile that never failed to dazzle.

'Thought you'd be busy out checking your newbies.'

He grinned. 'Seeing lambs born is close to magic. Taking their first shaky steps on long legs,' he shook his head, 'one of nature's many small miracles. But they're all doing fine. The sheep are in good condition and they're on fresh grass so the ewes are giving plenty of milk. Next thing you know we'll be shearing.'

'The fun never stops,' she quipped.

He graced her with a slow lazy smile. 'Something like that. Mack is out working on windmills today and won't be back until dark. Will I do?'

'Loaded question cowboy.'

Their gazes locked onto each other for a moment when she ached to be kissed but, without preamble, Mitch sauntered straight for her bike, hunkered down and scowled. 'Not looking good,' he muttered.

'It's a warning. Deliberate.'

'Mother said you don't want to report it.'

'No point.' She shrugged. 'No proof, only suspicion.'

Mitch rose. 'I'll go phone in the order so the tyres arrive tomorrow and we'll get these babies replaced.'

'Thanks.'

He stepped closer and reached out, rubbing the back of his hand against her arm. 'You should have someone close by at night.' His eyes studied her with warmth for a long while and the suggestion took a moment to digest.

'Tempting.'

He raised both arms. 'No strings. Purely protection.'

'That would be most…helpful and reassuring but I'll be fine.'

Standing astride, muscled legs packed into tight dusty jeans, hands on hips, Mitch Beaumont was tough to refuse but promise burned between them so she clung onto that thought.

'I'll give you a buzz when the tyres arrive.'

He'd already done that merely by his presence. 'Sure.'

'Take a few hours off and drive in with me in the morning? I'll throw in lunch at the pub and a beer.'

Darcy grinned. 'I'll think about it.' She already knew her answer but no point sounding too keen.

'See you tomorrow then.'

He hesitated and lingered then whistled to the dog investigating the edges of the waterhole, waited until it leapt back up onto the ute, fired up the vehicle and left.

Chapter 7

After Mitch's visit Darcy tried to focus and get back to work but he was a challenging man to ignore. Besides, her simmering fury over the bike tyres niggled her sense of fair play and stretched her tolerance.

She was fed up with sitting back and being stalked. Time for action. She would do a little chasing of her own. See how they liked that. When she had time, of course. She couldn't desert the dig. Maybe at night? Grab a few hours sometime when her tyres were fixed and she had wheels again. Get proactive and gather more information while she was out here. You never knew. One little piece of evidence could lead to another. She only needed to catch one break.

Mitch's phone call came late the following morning. She had already explained to the team the reason for her absence today and the vandalism revelation met with raised eyebrows and murmurs of alarm. On a rethink, she had changed her mind and told everyone because she wanted the whole team to stay alert. So she finished up her cataloguing to sprint to her tent and madly splash water on her face to freshen up. No time for a camp shower because he was already on his way in the ute when he phoned. No pressure.

Darcy released her dark hair from its pony tail, hastily flicked through with a brush before changing into clean cargos and tee shirt. He was gonna chuckle over the slogan on this one. It didn't mean anything, it was just a tease, but it was the first one she grabbed. She would watch Mitch's reaction with interest.

She had barely finished scrubbing up when he arrived. She tried to appear casual at the sight of his wavy sandy hair glinting in the crisp winter sunlight, Wranglers hugging that masculine body and his face wearing a special personal smile like he'd saved it just for her. When he eyed her warmly up and down with almost prized possession, it let Darcy know she was adored and she flooded with an equal responding appreciation. No man had ever walked into her life before and made such an impact.

Clearly, today was no time for hands off. Both felt heat for the other which Mitch satisfied with a long devastating kiss. If he hadn't been holding her so tight and close like they were a part of each other, she might just have buckled at the knees. When they broke apart, he held her at arm's length, his full gaze focused on her chest.

'How many of those do you have?'

She threw her head back and laughed. He meant the tee shirt, of course, not her boobs. Darcy sobered. 'Enough so I don't have to wash while I'm here.'

'Fair enough. Not big on housework.' He nodded at the words *I'd rather be carbon dating.* 'Hope that's not meant to keep me at bay 'cause I don't like your chances.'

She thrilled at his words. 'Just means I enjoy my work.'

'So…does this jaunt mean we're dating then?' he asked with guarded caution.

'You tell me.' She shrugged. 'You asked me along.'

'Cheeky. Do you *want* this to be a date?'

Darcy shook her head and chuckled. 'Let's just enjoy the ride today, okay?'

'Whatever you say.'

'Then take me away cowboy.'

Judging by Mitch's slow easy smile he understood her double meaning. One day. Hopefully soon.

Darcy could see he was equally rocked by their kiss and still feeling its effects when he stumbled and softly cursed while wheeling her motorbike up the ramp onto the back of the ute. Darcy idly leant against the lowered tailgate, hands in her pockets, admiring a strong man at work.

'You plan on helping?' he murmured.

'Nope. I'm just a simple country girl admiring the view.'

'Tease,' he growled from where he stood now on the ute tray looking down on her, having finally loaded Darcy's shiny bike.

He roped it down safe and tight then they jumped into the ute for the short trip back to the homestead. Mitch unloaded and rolled Darcy's motor bike into the workshop.

When he slid into the cab seat beside her again, he said, 'All set?'

She nodded. Although she suffered a measure of guilt for doing so, Darcy found the brief time away from the dig therapeutic. The lighter mood boosted by her companion too, of course. She had been focused so heavily on fossil *Mitch* and his importance, fearful of consequences since Hartley's betrayal and the Professor's appearance, that it was just so good to be bouncing along the rough dirt track across the station property heading for the main road into town with an occasional roo hopping across in front of them.

With her window wound down, the wind whistling through the cabin and country music on the radio life didn't get much better. She knew in the heat of summer this country would burn hot and dry before the annual drenching monsoon brought it back to life again. But today her heart filled at the sight of winter's breathtaking colours. Blue sky and green grasslands against the red of the outback soil and distant rocky escarpments.

As they turned onto the bitumen, there was no need for conversation. Beside her, Mitch's arm rested on his open window, the other lightly in control on the wheel. A light dust of sandy hair showed on his exposed arms below the rolled up shirt sleeves and sun browned skin.

'Almost afraid to ask but how was your parents' visit to Winton?'

'I understand they have more options now but need time to think them through.'

'Whatever they decide it will be a difficult decision and heavy responsibility.'

'For sure.' He paused. 'This tyre thing, you feeling nervous?'

'I'm too mad to be scared. When he insulted and tried to destroy me, Stirling made it personal. I'm convinced the Professor's involved. I mean, an older peer in our field of science with absolutely no regard for ethics? I'm not backing off. He just makes me more determined to catch him out.'

'How do you expect to get to the truth?'

'With difficulty,' she admitted over a sigh, 'but it's not impossible. Based on how close I've come in recent years and that his scare tactics mean I'm a serious threat, I've learned the most productive way is one-on-one tailing. So long as you believe you know the culprit,' she added wryly. 'Best crack at catching a fossil smuggler is red handed but in the outback, that means millions of acres. Plus Australia is ringed by coastline. Border patrols can't watch all of it all the time.'

Darcy shrugged and frowned as she explained. 'They could be using a remote airfield with poor security. Small planes and choppers can come and go and courier to a ship offshore maybe. There are dozens of possibilities. What I do feel for sure because my gut instinct tells me,' she continued with growing passion, 'is that Stirling is profiting from illegal fossil trading. I mean, the guy teaches at university. His salary might hit over six figures but geoscientists in oil and gas in places like Texas and Alaska earn bigger money.

'Yet Stirling lives on the Cullen Bay waterfront in Darwin. We're talking million dollar leafy private mansions with boats and private jetties. He either has a scary mortgage or he has other income. He doesn't often use his yacht except for an occasional spot of fishing but he takes regular holidays to Bali. I guess it's cheap so that figures but not the rest of his luxury lifestyle. Stirling doesn't like doing it tough. Most of the paleo guys I know prefer digging in dirt instead of sipping wine on a terrace.

'I've followed him to the airport and checked which flights he boarded. Wheedled out of his

PA where he stayed. Private Villa. All sounded legit. I tell you, I was so tempted to go along and conduct surveillance but time and money never allowed it.'

Mitch turned to her, his sandy hair tossed about by the cross breeze in the ute cabin. 'So theoretically he could be conducting business with his boss overseas?'

'Yeah,' Darcy groaned. 'That's been the one loophole bugging me all this time. My resources are limited.' She glanced across at him as he concentrated on the road ahead and Winton grew closer. 'You know, it's really nice to finally be able to talk to someone about this and not have them laugh or scoff in my face.'

'I'm stoked you trust me,' he said quietly.

'I've seen your fossil collection, remember?' she grinned. 'You're a fellow hunter.'

'And your mission to get Stirling has dominated your life.'

Darcy cringed at Mitch's assessment. 'True.'

'It's not wearing you down?'

'It's relentless,' she admitted, 'but I need to keep going until the end. Wherever that takes me.' Her gaze appealed for his understanding. 'I just need something definite. Anything. A confirmed meeting with his connection. A taped conversation, video. Solid evidence, you know? Information that will lead me directly to him. A day and time so I can pass it on to the authorities and they can follow it up and hopefully catch him in the act. I know I can only go so far and then it's up to the law but I need to get close to Stirling first and claim that one little link. Find out exactly when and where they transport the stuff.' Darcy gave a short laugh. 'Easy, huh?'

'Nothing worthwhile ever is,' Mitch said reasonably.

'Didn't figure it would take this long though.'

'You've been operating alone and on a budget. These guys sound loaded.'

'Black market's a lucrative business. An unscrupulous secretive world of criminals with powerful underground connections and backers in high places.'

'You've done your homework.'

'I've had plenty of time to watch and learn,' Darcy pulled a wry grin. 'I see my job as getting that breakthrough. Until I have something concrete to toss in front of the law, they won't listen. I jumped in too early the first time but I've kept my eyes and ears open ever since documenting it all in a diary. When I have that one vital thing – and I don't even know what that is yet – then the cops can track him or maybe entice him out into the open by setting up a sting.'

'Okay,' Mitch said slowly. 'Tell you what. I'll do all I can to help.'

Darcy's glance swung sharply in his direction, confirming he wasn't teasing. The slight dipping scowl on his forehead and focused gaze on the road told her he was serious and genuine. She drew in a deep breath, blown away by his offer.

'You have no idea what you're getting into.'

'Probably not,' he quipped, 'but everything within the law, right?'

'Of course,' she replied with sweet innocence.

He reached out and rested a hand over hers. 'I'm serious. We play by the rules, okay?'

Darcy nodded. 'Point taken.' There was too much to risk now to repeat her mistakes of the past.

Mitch's generosity was so huge, Darcy was nothing short of feeling so astounded and overwhelmed, she swallowed against the lump in her throat and threatening tears. He was still holding her hand and gave it a squeeze.

'Mitch,' she whispered, 'I can't-'

'I know. I can see it's time you end this. If I can play even a small part in that, I'm willing to give it a shot.'

'Thank you.' She furiously blinked back watery eyes and cleared her throat. 'Now, how much further is Winton? I'm starving and I need a beer.'

Mitch chuckled. 'You and me both. And about another five minutes.'

'Great.'

The one hour trip into town seemed shorter in Mitch's company. As Winton rose from the flat surrounding countryside, Darcy's thoughts reflected as they often did at the marvel that this dusty place was once part of a great inland sea. Hard to imagine now.

They cruised into town and slowed along the divided main street. Mitch reversed into the kerb to park in front of the same two storey hotel she had patronised on the day she arrived. Under the ground floor veranda tables and chairs were mostly filled with patrons. Above, the first floor balcony extended across the hotel front creating an imposing façade.

Darcy stretched after alighting from the ute and, together, she and Mitch strolled into the bar, the smell of beer and hum of conversation wafting into their senses.

It seemed like everyone in town was here. Mitch received slaps on the back, handshakes or a wave and smile of recognition from someone further away. And they weren't all mates. More than one female greeted him with familiarity, dreamy gazes lingering on Darcy's companion, surely one of the district catches. Their presence in town would be news. Word always spread. They took up two spare stools at the bar.

'So you found *Matilda Downs* all right then?' the bartender smiled, remembering her from a week ago.

To Darcy, so much had happened it seemed longer. 'Sure did. And I brought one of them back with me to prove it.'

'Mitch.' The barman greeted a fellow local. 'What brings you into town?'

'Motorbike tyres.' He didn't elaborate.

'What are you drinking?'

Both ordered a schooner of beer. As she sipped her icy amber drink, Darcy knew a comfortable feeling to be welcomed back, remembering the stairs at the far end leading to the first floor and the rows of gleaming glasses hanging from logs of wood above the bar. After a glance over the typical country menu chalkboard behind the bar with lots of steak options, Mitch chose a T-bone but Darcy opted for the barramundi, drawing out her memories of contented fishing days in the Territory, often on a camping trip with Grandpa Joe.

When the bartender moved on, Mitch indicated a spare table. 'Shall we make ourselves comfortable?'

'Sure.' Darcy slid off her stool bringing her beer and following him to be seated.

More than one glance strayed their way and she wondered how many people might have heard whispered gossip of a fossil find on *Matilda Downs*. She wasn't bothered that interested locals knew, only others with ulterior motives.

Their food arrived and they tucked into their generous lunch.

'You know, I love Dawnie's cooking but this seafood is the best,' Darcy confided, taking another draught of beer between mouthfuls of the sweet buttery flesh. 'There was no sport fishing in Grandpa Joe's little fibreglass tinny,' she reflected with a nostalgic smile. 'We mostly headed up the creeks and rivers to what he called his happy places. With the sun beating down out of a super blue sky that blazed pink and orange at the end of the day if we stayed out that late.'

'So, no Barra fishing, then?' Mitch grinned.

'We'd all have ended up in the water if we had. My brother Joe Junior always caught the most. I was just content to go along and drown a line.'

'Do you still go out?'

'Sometimes Joe, Dad and I go out when I'm home.'

When they finished eating, Mitch seemed keen to leave. Darcy grew consciously fascinated when they rose and every gaze in the bar followed them as they left the pub. And she felt even more charmed and special when he gently placed a hand in the small of her back guiding her to the ute.

'You're popular,' she quipped.

Mitch tossed her a wicked grin and drawled, 'Ever consider it might be the stunning woman with me?'

Darcy's heart lifted at his words. 'You'll get on.'

She was so distracted by Mitch's flirting and attentions, her brain sank into neutral until a showy black truck parked further along the street caught her eye.

She frowned. 'Is that Hartley's?'

Mitch half turned and followed her gaze. 'Possibly.'

Darcy was convinced. She recognised it instantly because it was so different. It stood out, which is exactly why the arrogant man owned it. Mitch's cool disinterested attitude didn't really puzzle her. His older brother seemed to be a disappointment all round.

Darcy couldn't imagine not laughing and teasing her own two brothers. Growing up, the siblings had shared everything together. On the rare times these days all the adult Mannings reunited, their camaraderie was as equally strong as it had been in their youth. They all had each other's back, no jealousies. They weren't perfect but they had all been raised to be respectful and granted that consideration to one another.

Hartley was obviously the black sheep that one heard about in families, despite a solid upbringing. So as Darcy climbed into the ute and clipped on her seat belt, her heart filled with sadness for Mitch who hadn't seemed to care that his brother was in town or made any effort to at least wave or stroll over and chat. The conversation may have been tense and uncomfortable anyway.

It wasn't until Mitch started up the ute and they moved out from their park at the kerb that

Darcy noticed two men standing at the back of Hartley's truck. Suddenly another cog in her mystery wheel of fossil smuggling investigations slipped into place. Here was her local link. Too obvious to ignore.

Judging by their body language, the Professor in pristine clothes – laughable in the outback – and Mitch's glowering brother, the two men as opposite as it was possible to be, were locked in what appeared to be a close intense conversation. Their demeanour and air of collusion and familiarity suggested they already knew each other and had previously met.

Hartley Beaumont and Professor Stirling.

It took Darcy a long moment to grasp the situation, unscramble her brain and recover her thoughts.

'So, Hartley still hasn't returned to *Matilda Downs*?' Darcy probed.

'No.'

'Then he wouldn't have met the Professor if he was out there because he's been away?'

'Yep.' Mitch glanced sideways, intrigued. 'Where is this going?'

'If you take a quick look in your rear view mirror you'll see them together.'

Mitch did as she suggested, scoffed, kept driving but turned the corner at the end of the main street and pulled over. He put the ute in park, leaving it idle, resting his hands on the steering wheel and staring straight ahead.

'Not good, huh?'

Both realised the implications of what the encounter signified. Too much to be coincidence. Based on the Professor's history and Hartley's dissatisfaction, the reality and likelihood of conspiracy was undeniable.

'Hart's betraying our family. Damn.' Mitch punched the wheel.

'You can bet Stirling did his research and sought your brother out.' Darcy reached out and rested a hand on his broad shoulder. 'I'm sorry.'

Mitch ground his jaw in determination. 'All the more reason to get to the bottom of all this. Get it sorted. I believe my parents' decision about the future of *Matilda Downs* is probably already made against Hart's favour but if we confirm your suspicions and get evidence, it might confirm their choice.' He scoffed with irony. 'My little fossil find might turn out to be more exciting and carry repercussions no one could have foreseen or planned.' He heaved out a long sigh. 'Might be time you told the folks about all this. What do you think?'

Darcy ached to see Mitch's agonised expression. She didn't hesitate to nod. 'Absolutely.' Ed and Nina Beaumont would be the souls of discretion and should be informed.

'Okay then, let's grab your motorbike tyres and we'll head back home.'

As they drove westward from town a short time later, Darcy's thought drifted. Mitch fell silent and equally reflective, no doubt contemplating his family situation. His brother's probable collusion with Stirling and disinterest in any involvement with the station property in any way. His parents must surely feel great strain over the recent happenings.

For such a genial hardworking couple with a situation beyond their control. Darcy hoped in time they could reconcile the eruption of events, deal with them and move on to happier family times.

Since Grandpa Joe's death, Darcy realised the importance of the elderly in a family, all too aware that her own parents were ageing too but still active and working. She made a purposeful promise to take some leave and go visit them in the Territory when this dig was done.

She allowed her gaze to wander from her open ute window and out across the sculpted ancient landscape, evident in the impressive flat-topped plateaus rising against the vast expanses of open grassland plans down here below.

Where Darcy and Mitch now travelled on their way back to the station, the Beaumont family oasis in the bush. But for how much longer she wondered?

She gained the impression that Mitch's younger brother Kit, spoken of fondly by his family, was a nomadic businessman. Their sister Elise was still at university. Who knew what future lay ahead for her? Mitch himself had his own property nearby.

It seemed questionable whether Hartley would ever shape up enough to be included in the station's future. He was a troubled man and unless he solved his own personal problems, not a comfortable favourite to lead *Matilda Downs* into the next generation.

Alongside the Beaumont family challenges, Darcy felt loaded with her own. After the harassment and personal vendetta from Stirling, resulting in massive life and career hiccups, for Darcy to see the Professor run free and unaccountable was a bitter pill to swallow.

With too many deliberately hidden facts, justice had certainly not been served to her satisfaction so her mission had begun and continued to this day.

'Penny for them,' Mitch said softly.

'As muddled as yours most likely.'

'One day at a time huh?'

'Yeah. We'll get through. Tough times don't last. Tough people do.'

They slowed and turned off the highway, following the rough red dirt track back across the station to the homestead. Mitch pulled up outside the workshop and made short work of unloading and rolling the new tyres into the shed alongside her bike.

Darcy slowly sauntered behind to watch the muscled man, shirt sleeves rolled up to the elbows and sighed. There was just something about a guy that could fix things. Should she tell him she'd done this before or stand aside and drool over the man who was quietly stealing her heart? Her sense of honesty and duty surfaced so she opted to help.

Mitch raised the bike up to remove the front wheel and lever the tyre loose. He removed the damaged tyre and tube, replaced them onto the rim and partly inflated the tube, inserting it back into the new tyre.

Darcy unbolted the back wheel ready for him to do the same and fixed the front one back on again while he worked on the second tyre.

'You're a handy woman to have around,' he murmured. 'Makes you a rather sexy lady.'

'Is that a problem for you?'

'Loving every minute,' he chuckled without looking up. 'Don't often see a woman in our workshop. Shows your strong sense of self-worth.'

'I may need to remind you of that one day.'

Awareness hummed around them like a swarm of native bees. They worked on in silence, finished the new tyres, fitting them back onto the bike.

Mitch replaced their tools and they both cleaned up in the wash basin installed at the rear of the workshop.

'Thanks,' Darcy said as Mitch lowered the jack and she wheeled her bike around. 'I'll take her for a spin and run them in.'

'Mind how you go and be careful then.' Mitch growled a friendly warning.

His concern and warm blue eyed gaze was disarming and, as always, set her heart racing just that little bit faster. 'I rode this baby from Darwin to Brisbane.'

'Just take every damn care, okay?' he said softly.

'Aww,' she flashed a teasing grin, 'course I will.'

Because he was standing there looking handsome and lost, and quite frankly too darned gorgeous to resist, she stepped closer, cupped his face in her hands and kissed his tempting mouth.

He responded instantly, of course, like he always did. With passion and possession. She was thrilled to know he wanted to own her. She would be his one day.

When the moment was right but not today. They sighed and reluctantly pulled apart.

It was crazy and presumptuous of her but Mitch Beaumont was the kind of country boy who made you realise who really mattered and always would. Each time they kissed, she tasted the possibility of a future with this humble sexy man.

And the look he sent in her direction pretty much told her he felt the same way, too.

Except for that mystery scowl on his face that she found unsettling and left her thoughts scrambled as she opened the throttle on her bike and rode away.

Chapter 8

As Mitch stood watching the country sweetheart of his dreams disappear down the dusty track on her motor bike heading for the waterhole and dig camp, his heart wrenched for the beautiful strong woman fighting a personal battle and struggling alone.

It was because of her very strength and resilience that his heart raged with anger and frustration for her, and his gut churned over with deep compassion until he knew he had to do something about it.

And to learn now that it appeared Hart was involved up to his neck, siding with Darcy's opposition, steamed him up even more. All hell was going to break loose on the Beaumont home front now it was known his brother was tangled up with Stirling's mob.

They needed definite proof of course but when they did and if their suspicions checked out, his deepest wish for Darcy was that the fossil smuggling ring be cracked, supporting her claims after all these years. Only then would she get her life back and move on. He just hoped she wanted him to be a part of it. If she needed convincing, he would be open to a little persuasion.

At this point and when he offered, he had absolutely no idea how much help he could possibly be to Darcy but he would be guided by her lead and do whatever she asked to get the job done. See what they could come up with.

One notion came to mind. A long shot but worth a try. He didn't plan on telling Darcy in case it came to nothing.

Mitch strolled over to the homestead to use the landline and have a discussion over smoko with his parents. The news he was about to convey would hardly be welcome and he hated being the bearer because it would only add to the stress load they were under at the moment.

They took it well, exclaimed in alarm over Darcy's bike tyres now they knew the cause and asked after her wellbeing with deep concern.

After he had knocked back two cups of tea and a slab of his mother's favourite fruit cake, Mitch excused himself to give them time to digest the information and suspicions he and Darcy shared about Hart to make his phone call from the homestead office. They were gonna need help and he knew just the man. A lawyer mate and long-time friend from university, experienced in court work and litigation.

'Mitch, great to hear from you. What's happening mate?'

Despite his eminent position as one of the major partners in his own law firm, Glenn Whyte was a down to earth genuine guy. With one very clever brain. Mitch planned to make use of it.

'I know you're always busy mate but I need to call in a favour.' He briefly explained the situation, scooting over the basics.

'Happy to help,' Glenn said easily. 'Best get yourself on a plane and come down to Brisbane so we can talk about it.'

Mitch booked a flight from Longreach for the following morning and an overnight motel east of town near the airport three hours away. He packed a bag and was on the road after a quick explanation to his parents and instructions to keep an eye on Darcy.

'No idea how long I'll be gone. I'll keep in touch,' he said.

On the ride back to the waterhole and camp, Darcy was still haunted over Mitch's frown and distraction when she left him at the workshop. Unlike him to look blue.

She re-joined the dig team on site for the last working hours of the day before the team broke for dinner and another camp fire chat.

Restless, Darcy excused herself and while she still had an hour of daylight to play with, followed a crazy hunch. She grabbed a sandwich from Dawnie in the catering tent and stowed her camera in the side bag on her bike. For the second time that day she travelled into Winton, the sun just setting as she rumbled into town.

Keeping a low profile and in a low gear, she casually cruised the streets seeking out either of the two men she had seen earlier. Instinct told her not to stray too far from the same pub but she dare not reveal herself by going inside. Instead, she kept circling town, her patience eventually rewarded when her adversary and another man she didn't recognise emerged from the pub while she ate her sandwich in the poorly lit shadows on the opposite side of the street.

The two men headed for a white four wheel drive and the road west from town. Darcy clipped on her helmet and followed.

On this flat open country with no cover against detection, Darcy wasn't game to even risk being seen by turning on parking lights so, once she was out of town, she killed her headlights and rode with only the centre line cat's eyes to light her way in the dark.

Fortunately the country road was quiet with little other traffic and she kept her distance from the vehicle ahead. About ten clicks out of town it turned off the highway and headed north toward the jump up.

Darcy suspected a meeting place. Despite the danger of discovery, she needed to follow. The fact they were taking such careful precautions way out here in this isolated spot suggested they were getting serious or at the least the rendezvous was important. That fact alone urged her to continue the pursuit.

At the turn, she took care there was no immediate sign of the vehicle ahead except the distant red tail lights.

At least some measure of camouflage and protection developed in the landscape here. The Mitchell grass plains became a light woodland of spinifex and small ghost gums. She trailed them on the stony track halfway up the escarpment until they suddenly stopped. Swiftly, Darcy cut her engine, hid her bike behind rocks and sought cover. She might have to wait until they left later before doing so herself for fear of discovery.

If she learned something new she would watch and wait for as long as it took. She could lie low until this subterfuge was over. But in her experience these secret meetings rarely lasted long.

A low roll of excitement churned her stomach at the thought that, maybe this time, she might glean that one single thread of evidence against the Professor to prove her innocence from five years ago and that the man was still smuggling fossils, no doubt for good money. Lucky bugger just hadn't been caught. Yet. Darcy hoped to change that.

Keeping low and crawling closer, Darcy

peered around a huge boulder. The road had opened out into a small canyon and Hartley's truck was already parked there, waiting. All three men cut their lights, left the vehicles and stood in a huddle, talking. The sounds of their deep voices carried on the night air bouncing off the cliff walls but she needed to get nearer to hear what they were actually saying.

Holding her breath and treading carefully with each step she took, praying no stones rolled under her boots to give away her presence, Darcy edged only near enough to eavesdrop on the conversation.

Stirling introduced Hartley and the stranger to each other. Sounded like *Bennie* or *Bernie*. No surname. Damn. In the glow of the one torch Hartley carried, Bennie gestured further along behind them to what looked like a narrow corridor between the high sided rocks.

As they turned their backs and walked in the other direction, Darcy managed to sneak across to the cover of their vehicles, hearing the echo of Stirling's voice say something like *a trial run* as they disappeared.

Darcy heaved out a sigh of frustration and wrinkled up her nose in disappointment. There was no cover for her down there. She must stay put. Before she retreated though and because they were walking away not looking at her, Darcy braved standing up. She gasped. Hartley's torch flashed around the interior and sides of what appeared to be a cave.

She scrambled back up the slight stony rise again to crouch down behind the boulder near her bike, took photos from the better vantage point, cursing her luck but noting down the number plate of the four wheel drive.

This meeting better mean *something*. Maybe Stirling was planning a small steal before the main one? Knowing the man well, whatever his intentions they were unlikely to be legal.

As she sat alone in the dark, Darcy longed to hear their conversation but the rocky terrain and exposure in the open gorge made it impossible to risk being detected. She could stumble, be hurt, discovered. What she had gathered from this stake out and location tonight must build to more clues.

In her frustration, time crawled but it was probably only about five or ten minutes before the men returned. Darcy flattened herself to the ground, peering on her stomach through a rock fissure to try and glimpse what they were doing.

Apparently discussions were over. Stirling and Bennie backed up in the four wheel drive until they had more space for a three point turn. When their headlights swept exactly where Darcy lay, she froze and stopped breathing. But moments later it turned back down the track toward the main road. Hartley's throaty truck reversed, turned and followed.

When all lights had faded, Darcy waited in

complete darkness for ages until her heartbeat slowed and she was confident enough to leave. She only put the bike parking lights on and drove slow, barely above idle, to reduce her engine noise that echoed across the silent scrub as though she had it on full throttle.

At the highway intersection with no vehicles in sight in either direction, she took to the tarmac again and sped back out toward the turn off to *Matilda Station*.

The man in the truck smoked a cigar and deliberated over the tantalising offer the boss had just made him. He jerked to high alert at the sound of a low throbbing engine coming up behind him on the rough track leading away from the jump up where he had just met Stirling and Bernie, out to make some quick decent money like himself.

After the other men left, he had swung off the red dirt road into the bush to consider his options and the promised ongoing financial rewards of an alliance with the syndicate. Easier money than chasing sheep and lots more of it.

Hell, Mitch might be foolish enough to waste his time out here in this Godforsaken country but he had other plans for his own life and getting rich. He saw a different life for himself than farming. He didn't give a damn about *Matilda Station* and even less about being the oldest son and heir expected to love it and carry on some lousy family tradition.

So with his relaxed mind deep in thought and the heavenly aroma of an occasional puff of smoke drifting around him and out through his open window, his body tensed but his mind stayed cool. Who cared what people thought of him out here at this time of night skulking in the dark? If the Professor had put a tail on him he'd regret it. He had nothing to hide. He was just thinking. Had good reason, too. Lots to consider. No law against that.

So he relaxed as the vehicle grew closer until a motor bike slowly rolled past and his visual radar hit the alarm button. Damn but he would recognise the woman on that shiny machine even in the dark. He swore to himself at her sly spying, the damage she could do to their operation and the repercussions for everyone. His hard mouth curled into a smirk of pleasure. This development was ripe for blackmail. He would pay the interfering snoop a little visit. On the quiet, like.

As Darcy returned to *Matilda Station* and the dig camp site, weary with tension, she felt only relief to have escaped the jump up bush rendezvous unseen. But frustrated she had heard little, seen even less and only grabbed some quick photos and a vehicle number plate.

Convinced the Professor had some kind of action planned, she knew she needed more information. Somehow with working all day on the dig, she had to find it.

She tried to steady her irritation by stoking her camp fire and boiling the billy for a cuppa. Sitting enveloped by the night and its sounds, hugging her enamel tea mug, Darcy let her gaze slide over the shadowed waterhole and above to the vast starlit sky.

This combination of peace, nature and endless skies, day *and* night, sucked you in like a habit you couldn't break. Not seeing another person was actually exhilarating. It showed up the vastness and power of millions of years of creation. Having been born in the north, the outback would always be in her soul.

It would have been awesome if Mitch had been here waiting for her. She wished. When she closed her eyes she was with him. So far she had only experienced the heavenly luxury of a few moments in his arms but she knew without question he was most likely the only man who would ever remain in her heart. That this phenomenon should strike her with such intensity and after only a week since their first meeting back at the homestead, simply blew her mind.

Staring into the low flames, she even considered the crazy chance that they might make their lives work together. Mitch out here on the sheep station, she digging up and identifying fossils all over the country. At least she had done in the past. But since outback Queensland was becoming dinosaur central she wouldn't need to stray far though, would she?

She pulled herself from idle daydreams, her eyelids heavy. Instead she crept into her sleeping bag and snuggled down considering possibilities and imaginary wild romantic longings.

In the following days, the dig advanced. Into their second week, the team had excavated further down and unearthed yet more bones, making this one of the most productive sites on which Darcy had ever worked. Even more astonishing was the fact they were all handling a carcass undisturbed since death hundreds of millions of years before.

She felt beyond excited about each new discovery, no matter how small. Fossil fragments were often part of a larger bone and their jigsaw pieces would be put together back at the lab.

Any day now Darcy would help train the team on covering their main fossil *Mitch* with its plaster cap. It would dry to a hard shell of protection before they carefully rolled him over to do the other side.

Two days later it was time for the whole team's big day off. An excursion into Winton and the Australian Age of Dinosaurs museum south west of town. Later they would take a tour to the jump up for a picnic lunch with spectacular views before returning to the dig by sunset for a welcome shower and their usual happy hour.

Two of the men generously offered to stay behind as on-site watch for the day. Darcy was pleased not to be left alone for she had excused herself from joining the outing, planning to use the time to catch up on labelling and laptop work as well as one of her regular detailed reports back to the museum.

In the back of her mind later on when her business was done, she also hoped to ride back to the homestead. She hadn't heard anything from Mitch which seemed strange. He at least sent her texts or came out to the dig or her camp site to see how it was all going.

His absence was baffling and she missed him. Plus she was burning to tell him where she went the other night on her bike after they had jointly changed the tyres in the workshop, about the smugglers' rendezvous and his brother's definite deep involvement.

So by late afternoon, her wish was granted. With work done, she cleaned up under the camp solar shower, washed her long hair and sat brushing it dry before the fire. Not much choice of clothes but she managed a clean pair of black jeans and a soft chambray shirt. For once, no tee shirt and dinosaur slogan. She wanted this visit tonight to be special.

She tugged on her short tan boots and shrugged on her black leather jacket.

As she kicked her bike into life and rumbled along the station track heading into the golden evening sunset, Darcy hoped this late in the day she might be the beneficiary of Nina and Ed's remembered warm hospitality. Invited into the homestead for a drink or even dinner, although Dawnie would have a huge meal prepared for the dig crew when they returned.

But her stomach flipped over with promise just at the likelihood of seeing Mitch again. She usually didn't put herself out there like this so her efforts left her feeling vulnerable and insecure.

Her heart and spirits lifted even higher to see the homestead come into view, its welcoming lights on, glowing out into the descending dusk.

She parked her bike out front and hung her helmet over the handlebars, took a deep breath and ran lightly up the broad steps onto the veranda. She rapped on the timber fame of the wire screen door, the inner door open and giving a view down the long central hallway.

Darcy frowned. The usual movement and noise from previous visits was missing. Something wasn't right. She discovered exactly what when an unwelcome sight stepped into view, a can of beer in one hand and a cigar in the other.

Her mood dropped and her heart skipped beats. Damn. Hartley was back. Okay, a snag to bear for the evening. Her stomach twisted into knots as he strolled aggressively toward her, clearly bolstered even more than his usual arrogant self by the alcohol. She was doubly surprised to even see him in this house because from Mitch's account, his brother usually kept to himself in his own cottage.

She couldn't have picked a worse time to call. If not for the expectation of seeing Mitch tonight, she would have returned to camp. But she could do this. Be fake.

Unsmiling but polite, Darcy said crisply, 'Hartley.'

He responded with a superior grin, leaning a shoulder against the wall looking threatening. 'Well, well, well. If it isn't the Doctor. You've saved me a trip.'

He intended coming out to see her? Why? Every alarm rattled in her brain.

'I've come to see Mitch.'

'Have you now?

'He chuckled and Darcy grew impatient not to at least be invited in. She glanced over his shoulder. Where was Mitch or his parents? Hartley delayed. Huge doubts crept into Darcy's mind causing a roll of panic in her stomach.

'Well,' Hartley said eventually, 'you're just gonna have to make do with me tonight.'

'I'm sorry?' Darcy scowled.

'I'm not.' Hartley scanned every inch of her body from her freshly washed hair swinging about her shoulders and back to her polished boots. 'Mitch has gone AWOL.'

Darcy's excitement had long died. He had? He'd not said anything to her. Was Hartley lying? Maybe Mitch had urgent business.

'Folks wouldn't tell me where,' he went on, then paused and his stare narrowed. 'Everyone seems to have their secrets lately.'

'Do they?'

Darcy caught her breath and tried to appear unconcerned, act casual. Not let this creepy man get to her but his last words had sounded like a threat.

'The olds are at some function in town. Won't be back until *real late*,' he drawled.

Winton was an hour away so the Beaumonts might not return until midnight. What to do? How to escape this situation. She was only steps from her bike. She could leave. Then her assurance slowly returned and her stunned brain cleared.

She might learn more if she stayed but could she endure and manipulate this repulsive man to do it?

Hartley stuck the cigar in his mouth and opened the wire door. 'Come in and partake of Beaumont hospitality. Get better acquainted.'

Darcy felt like a fly about to be caught in a spider's web. She knew the risk if she accepted the offer but she could look after herself. She'd done it a time or two before in sticky situations with forward outback boys hungry for female company.

For a fleeting moment she had second thoughts, then nodded. 'Sure. I could handle a drink.'

As she stepped over the threshold and brushed past Hartley's hops-ridden smoky body, it was with caution, fully understanding that tonight she was not entering the Beaumont family homestead in normal circumstances but an enemy's lair, as vigilant and prepared as she could be.

Chapter 9

Mitch yawned as he settled back on yet another flight and stared out at the blue sky as they flew above the clouds. Hopefully the last leg of his search, each getting closer than the last.

He couldn't believe how much he had achieved with Glenn's dynamic help. The guy didn't mess around. He knuckled down and got into it. Over the past two days, his mate knew the right person to contact, called them, set up appointments and made stuff happen.

Just last night before flying back to Brisbane, Glenn had given him a few vital tips for interviewing a key witness which Mitch hoped this man turned out to be. Then he could return to Darcy with good news. He needed to gain this guy's trust with the aim of getting information and results as efficiently as possible.

Mitch now knew why Glenn operated that way. He simply didn't have any free time. He needed to get the job done and a result for his client. That his mate was doing all this pro bono blew him away. Even chalked up all their flights to business expenses.

Mitch didn't enjoy all this international jet setting. He would rather keep his boots firmly on the ground, preferably in red outback dirt. But he had a damn good reason and she was digging up dinosaurs on *Matilda Downs.*

As he endured the two and a half hour flight from Darwin to Indonesia, his mind idly clicked back over his hectic recent days. Glenn lived and worked under pressure and thrived on it. Mitch soon learned to keep up!

He grinned to himself as he accepted a drink from the flight attendant, reflecting on that first meeting with his mate.

Mitch had gaped at the floor to ceiling window views from his office overlooking the Brisbane River. He'd whistled as he'd entered and Glenn had chuckled. Not your usual suited lawyer though which didn't make Mitch feel too out of place in his cargoes and black tee shirt.

Glenn greeted him in jeans and an open necked white shirt with a big bear hug and slap on the back that resonated with his usual genuine warmth. No tie in sight. It had been a while but their reunion was casual, easy and instantly settled into their old jovial friendship.

Mitch didn't waste time. Glenn had none to spare but this smart lawyer was a deadly smooth operator in his professional domain yet possessed the biggest heart in the world. As best he could, Mitch briefly explained Darcy's experience in Darwin five years before and the current situation and happenings.

Glenn frowned and listened. When Mitch finished, he said, 'Okay, let's do this.'

Within minutes he had online access to the Northern Territory database of court decisions.

'Hmm, before a judge, deemed insufficient evidence to proceed,' Glenn muttered and looked up. 'Case dismissed. No surprise there.' He logged out of the website, leaned back in his leather chair and tented his fingers. 'You trust your woman's instincts?'

'She's not my woman.'

'Doesn't mean you don't want her to be,' Glenn flashed a teasing grin.

He was happily married to a tolerant organised redhead called Simone who juggled raising three kids with a part time medical career of her own. Each time they met again, Glenn never let an opportunity pass hinting that Mitch needed the same.

'Stop playing around with sheep, mate, and settle down.'

'Working on it.'

He flickered his thick dark eyebrows. 'You've never said that before. Sounds promising.'

'In answer to your question,' Mitch said earnestly, hoping to ditch the teasing and direct their conversation back on track. 'Yes I absolutely trust Darcy's instinct. If you met her you'd agree.'

'Look forward to it.' Glenn leant forward, clasping his hands together on his desk, surprisingly tidy for a busy man. 'Then we need to fly to Darwin, mate, to check out the court library and go over every piece of paper we can find.'

'How the hell are you gonna manage that?'

Glenn shrugged. 'They're open to the legal profession with prior permission. I'll arrange it.'

And he did. As well as the four hour flight to get there. And instructions to his PA to cancel or shuffle his calendar until he returned.

'Hell, Glenn. You have time for this?'

'Nope but nothing's achieved by sitting on your hands.'

Later that same day they were landing in Darwin adjusting to its sticky tropical heat and the next morning found both men in the court library as soon as it opened wading through all the paper files and records of the investigation five years ago that had so affected and changed Darcy's life. And not for the better.

Just after they had stopped for lunch, Glenn said suddenly, 'Might have found a chink, mate. We need to follow this up.'

Mitch accepted the papers and read with interest. The declaration was startling. Darcy had never mentioned anything about this. Maybe she didn't know.

'Okay, it's a clue but how is this important?'

'It was taken down but never used or presented as evidence. If the lawyer's had followed this up and acted on it, Stirling should have been investigated further. Clearly, nothing happened.' He shared a long glance with Mitch. 'Money changed hands?'

'Shit.' Mitch stood up, pacing, rubbing his tired eyes. 'This little guy could be the link Darcy keeps mentioning.'

'Sure have to wonder what happened to him. We need to find him and see if he would stand up in court.'

After a pile of photocopying that Glenn shoved in his bulky briefcase, the men headed for the university office.

With his legal clout, they were given the man's records.

Reading them, Mitch shook his head in disgust. The Indonesian man, Bima, left the university employ days after giving his statement. His file indicated his return home to Indonesia. With an address.

'I need to get back to Brisbane, mate,' Glenn said. 'You're it.'

Mitch refocused as the overhead cabin speakers announced their landing. The hot sub-tropical air hit as he left the airport and hailed a taxi.

He was beat but smelt success. It wasn't in the bag yet but the cleaner, Bima, had been detailed and honest in his statement which gave Mitch encouragement and a positive feeling of hope.

Because Darcy totally distrusted him, she watched Hartley knock back the rest of his can of beer then pour them each a shot of brandy into chubby crystal glasses from a matching decanter on the living room sideboard. She accepted it and took a mouthful of spirits that burned a path of courage as it slid down.

Darcy felt bad for feeling so uncomfortable around Mitch's brother but a girl could never be too careful.

Hartley circled her and said smoothly, 'So, you have a thing going with my little brother?'

'He's a good bloke,' Darcy said crisply, having no intention of being agreeable.

'And I'm not?' he growled, moving closer, his voice lowered, his words already beginning to slur.

Good, Darcy thought with pleasure and optimism. When arrogant drunks grew annoyed, they often spat out the truth to prove themselves. Darcy was tall and strong, a woman who had lived a physical outdoor life but while Hartley Beaumont might be an emotionally weak, he was powerfully built so she needed to stay alert. His words and actions were sinister but she had no intention of pushing him too far.

He stroked the back of his hand along her arm. 'You should cooperate or it will be worse for you.'

Darcy frowned, unsure what he meant. A threat. Why? 'I'm only here in my professional capacity to work on the dig site.'

'Oh, we both know you're interfering way more than that.' He leaned close, his foul breath blowing against her cheek as he whispered in her ear, 'Enjoy your little ride in the bush the other night?'

Darcy chilled to the bone, mad with anger. He'd seen her? He'd given no sign when the men were all in the canyon and she was watching them. Must have been later. As she left?

'I was just testing my bike tyres after they were slashed.' She narrowed her gaze on him, knowing exactly who was responsible.

'A chick alone? Miles from anywhere? In the dark?' he sneered. 'We both know it was more than that.'

Okay so *he* knew but did the others? Tonight felt like blackmail, a squeeze. Her silence and obedience? Fat chance.

When she deliberately didn't answer he pulled a superior grin, believing he had the upper hand. Let him relax a little, Darcy thought. Drop his guard and maybe back off. She could handle a pompous drunk but not an aggressor. So she tried a different tack.

'It's not too late to back out, Hartley.' For a moment she could see her words raised a flicker of attention.

'You don't get it. I don't want to. This is my way out.'

'You're in deep with Stirling but if you help the authorities, they'll do a deal. Go easy on you. Co-operate with them?' she pleaded, softening her voice as though she was concerned for him.

He barked out a short laugh. 'I don't rat on my mates.'

'Yet you've betrayed your family by siding with a criminal against them,' she snapped back.

He scoffed. 'This property is worth millions but it's all in land and I'm not interested. I won't be stuck out here much longer.'

Only if he got away with it. 'You could have the guts to tell your parents.'

He sneered. 'I'm sure they've guessed. I want a better life than this and I'll get it when they pay me.'

'Don't be so sure. Stirling doesn't let the truth get in the way of a dollar. I challenged him and he framed me. Be careful. He's loyal to no one.'

'Sour grapes. He's told me all about you.'

'His version I'm sure.'

'I don't give a damn. I'm only after the money. And you won't be getting in our way.'

He glowered at her, swallowed the rest of his drink and poured himself another, draining it all in one huge swill. Darcy left a portion of hers in the glass. Might come in handy if she needed to throw it in his face.

He swaggered over to her again and shoved

his unshaven face close. 'Back off or you'll regret it.'

Darcy glared at him, her body growing more tense with every moment that passed. 'Brave words but I'm not afraid of you.'

He suddenly lashed out and gripped her arm, his steely fingers digging deep into her flesh. 'You should be.'

Okay, Hartley had crossed a line. Touching without her permission was assault. Especially this aggressive. But now he'd sunk to coercion, trying to break her through fear and threats. She refused to give any sign that she was in pain. But Darcy was alarmed at his swift turn of mood from conceited insolence to hostile force. She gritted her teeth and squirmed to get free.

'Only weak men use violence on a woman. Let me go.'

'Not until you promise to keep your mouth shut, do your job and leave. No more prowling around or I'll tell the boss.'

So, Stirling didn't know! A major piece of information in her favour. 'No!' she bit out in sharp defiance.

He shook her. 'Agree or I'll scar that pretty face and neck for life.'

The situation was growing serious. She couldn't afford to let it escalate. Time for action. But what? How to pacify him? As she scrambled to be free, she flung the brandy in his face. He cursed, closed his eyes and shook his head to clear the liquid but didn't let her go.

Instead, his anger rose. 'Promise,' he bellowed, his eyes gleaming with malice.

'Stop it, Hartley. This is crazy. I won't change my mind. You're making it worse for yourself. This is assault.'

On a pin prick of hope, Darcy deliberately raised her voice. She could have sworn she heard a sound outside. Then, as though she watched in slow motion, Hartley reached into his pocket and produced something, pressed a button and it snapped open.

'Promise,' he roared.

Shit. A flick knife. Life just got super real. Darcy was just about to try and raise her knee to kick him where it would hurt but Hartley caught her off balance, twisted her arm behind her back, pulled her hard up against him and held the blade to her throat. Darcy wisely froze in fear, knowing any movement would be critical and come with dire consequences.

In the silence of their gasping and ragged breathing, Hartley stiffened. He had heard it too. An approaching vehicle with a flash of lights as it swung to a stop in front of the homestead. He cursed low under his breath. Darcy sensed his indecision. He was trapped but if he continued to hold her fast, whoever came through that door would be an eye witness. Whoever had arrived, she was just grateful for their timing and that help and intervention had come.

But was it in time? It only took a second to use a knife.

The vehicle lights snapped off, a door slammed, dogs barked and light footsteps ascended the front steps. Darcy's heart sank. Didn't sound heavy enough for a man's tread. Maybe it was Nina?

Within seconds, a young blonde woman breezed into the hallway. Darcy felt Hartley's arm lower from her throat and heard the flick knife retract, returned to his pocket. With one hand free from holding her, she tried squirming to cut loose from his agonising grip but he refused to release her.

Seeing them together through the open living room doorway, the girl flashed a sharp and knowing blue-eyed glance between Darcy and Hartley, struggling against each other. The overnight bag slid from her shoulder and thumped on the floor.

She planted her hands on her hips. Darcy sensed that behind her petite persona, lay an iron will. And she looked so like Mitch, this pocket dynamo could only be his sister Elise, home unexpectedly from university in Brisbane perhaps? Darcy almost laughed with ironic relief that her saviour should turn out to be this tiny person. Who was the image of what her attractive mother would have been forty years ago.

'What the hell's going on here?' Her voice was

strong and melodic.

Darcy cast her a desperate pleading gaze. The girl's eyebrows rose slightly and her attention immediately focused on her brother.

'Hart?' she growled, a cutting glare directed at him as she took a cautious step in from the hallway.

Darcy felt Hartley breathing heavily, fuming with rage beside her as he reluctantly surrendered control and stepped aside.

She hastily scrambled to compose herself. Did only she and Hart know he had threatened her with a weapon? If so it would be his word against hers. Or had Elise glimpsed something?

'I came to see Mitch,' Darcy gasped in a ragged voice. 'Your brother's *hospitality*,' her mouth curled in irony, 'was overwhelming.'

Elise strode fully into the living room. ''Wouldn't be the first time.' She bypassed Darcy and shook Hartley's arm. 'You're drunk again! Hell, Hart, you've been warned. Mum and Dad will hear about this.'

'Just having a little fun.' Hart slurred his words as he spoke, the alcohol finally taking its toll.

'We all know your idea of *fun*. Didn't look like our guest was enjoying it.' She turned to Darcy. 'Are you okay?' she asked, a genuine note of regret in her voice.

'Yes, fine. Considering.' She extended a hand. 'Darcy Manning. I'm leading the team working out on the fossil dig site. You have to be Elise.'

She managed a shaky smile, still unsettled from her horrific encounter with Hartley. A hand drifted up to her throat where moments earlier the cold blade of his knife had pressed against her skin with terrifying reality.

'Got it in one.' Elise shook her hand warmly, continually glancing toward her brother, checking that he was no longer any serious danger to either of them.

Pathetically Darcy now noticed Hartley floundered uselessly, his abilities clouded. A sorry sight with an ugly edge.

'My parents have mentioned you,' Elise said. 'I caught up with them in Winton on my way through. They're not far behind. Be home soon. I'm sorry Mitch wasn't here.'

'I was just going to update him on the latest dig information.'

Elise reached out and gently placed a hand on Darcy's arm. 'Are you sure you're all right?'

Scowling, she glanced over Elise's shoulder. Hartley had slumped onto a sofa, probably unable to stand up any longer. He'd been unsteady on his feet before but, unfortunately, still enough in control of his faculties and his knife to cause Darcy some serious heart stopping moments.

'Yes, I'm okay. Thanks. I'll just use the bathroom.' She needed time alone to process what had just happened, try and stop this trembling and gather her poise. 'I know where it is,' she vaguely gestured.

'Sure. Then we'll talk. I'll boil the kettle.'

Chapter 10

Darcy shook all over as she closed the bathroom door and locked it behind her, leaning back against it taking deep deliberate breaths to steady her fast beating heart. Until she was alone in the quiet and away from the drama, she hadn't realised it was racing.

It was useless to consider it but she wondered whether to blame herself for accepting Hartley's loaded invitation into the homestead. Had she been too over confident? But who knew he had that knife stashed in his pocket?

All very well to hold ambition to get ahead in life but to physically bully and endanger another person to achieve it was unforgiveable. And illegal. But then Hartley Beaumont didn't appear to be friends with the law.

Darcy wasn't sure she could let tonight's incident pass. She didn't want to cause trouble in the family but their son was a seriously cruel alcoholic who needed help. From what Elise hinted, she gathered something similar had happened before. Clearly he was on a destructive path and if his behaviour was allowed to continue unchecked, Darcy shuddered to think what could happen.

As she splashed warm water on her face and dabbed it gently dry with a soft fluffy hand towel, it was impossible not to overhear the raised voices that carried to her from the lounge.

'Did I see a knife?' she heard Elise ask.

Yes! Darcy screamed to herself in relief. She *had* seen something. Hartley mumbled an incoherent reply.

'Now! Or I'll phone Dad.' A pause. 'No. You sit right there. Move and I'll call the police and we'll make this official. Gimme your truck keys. Keys!" she repeated louder, 'or I'll get a rifle from the office. In your condition I'll have it loaded and trained on you before you reach the front door.'

'Don't be stupid.'

'I've never been stupid and you know it.'

'You wouldn't dare.'

'Push me,' she challenged. Silence for a moment. 'No more. This stops now,' she said in a gentler voice edged with resignation.

Darcy was surprised that such stern words came from such a slim young thing. Clearly a fellow woman of the outback. No bullshit and she sure could handle her brother. She heard

Hart's pathetic pleading and when her own name was mentioned once or twice, she flinched. Probably lies. She hoped Elise didn't believe him.

Darcy regrouped, eyed off her startled returning image in the mirror, combed fingers through her hair and gradually felt calmer even if she didn't look it. Taking more deep breaths, she re-emerged.

Hart sat sullen on the sofa, head back, eyes closed. Elise paced in front of him as she crisply talked on the home phone in low tones. Seconds later she wrapped up her conversation, noticed Darcy standing in the doorway and asked, 'Feeling better?'

'I'll be fine but your family needs to take action,' said with blunt honesty.

Hartley recovered enough to open his eyes and glare at her, scowling. Darcy rubbed her arms and moved closer, remaining in the kitchen but forcing herself to confront him.

In a quiet voice as controlled as she could muster under the circumstances, she said, 'Just for the record, I expect bullshit from men like you but I never accept it. And by the way, it's never okay to be cruel and certainly not to use male power and take advantage of a woman. I hope karma slaps you in the face real soon. Save me doing it. Frankly, you're not worth the energy.'

'You'll be sorry about this. You don't know

what you've done.'

'Hart!' Elise snapped. 'Save it. Your future is not looking good.'

She turned to Darcy. 'Come into the kitchen. I make a mean coffee,' she grinned. When Darcy hesitated and glanced in Hart's direction, she said, 'My dogs are at the door and I'm only steps from Dad's rifle. He's not going anywhere.'

A young thing with all the answers. Darcy was just grateful Elise had arrived and, knowing her brother well, taken charge.

Darcy followed Elise into the gigantic country kitchen where she had been so warmly welcomed sitting around its scrubbed central table the first day she arrived. And had met Mitch. Mitch. Darcy inwardly groaned. What would he think of all this?

She couldn't help glancing nervously to the half-closed French doors that led back to the adjoining sitting room.

'Relax. He's still snoring and my boys at the front door will let me know if he moves.' Elise said with firm reassurance. 'Folks will be here any second.'

She moved around the kitchen making coffee so Darcy took a seat.

Elise lowered her voice, 'I'm so sorry you had to suffer this. The family have had reports on the grapevine this past year. There have been one or two *incidents*. Brawls and drinking. He's my brother,' she shrugged. 'It breaks my heart but no one has filed a complaint.'

'Maybe it's time they did,' Darcy said with conviction.

Elise nodded. 'We'll understand if you do.'

'I was afraid for my life tonight, Elise. If you hadn't arrived and with Hartley off his face-', Darcy caught her breath. 'Your family should think about that.'

'I know. I'm truly sorry.'

'I'm sure you all are but that doesn't help him. Seems to me Hartley's a danger to himself and the community. You need to face facts and stop protecting him.'

'He's never gone this far before,' Elise protested.

'He has now.'

Darcy's blunt words about Hartley's assault and behaviour caught Elise by surprise and neither spoke for a long time. Tension filled the air in the kitchen as she rustled about with cuppa preparations.

For Darcy, the realisation of what could have been her fate tonight was starting to hit home and she felt queasy in nervous reaction.

So she just listened when, after a while in a subdued reflective tone, Elise sighed. 'Now the folks are getting older, they're keen for one of us to start the next generation with grandkids and heirs, you know? My brothers are all late starters and dragging their feet,' she half smiled wryly. 'Although Hart will be a challenge for any woman until he sorts himself out.'

'Do you believe that will happen?'

'I hope so. Beaumonts have been on *Matilda Downs* since my great grandparents Matilda and Eli settled here in the late 1800s. Naturally as the oldest first born, Hart was the usual choice to carry it on but that ain't gonna happen,' she attempted another grin. 'Beside his personal problems, he's not a leader to take this station into the future.'

Elise set two mugs of steaming aromatic coffee on the table, placing milk and sugar between them.

'Mitch keeps his heart close,' Elise went on, 'so who knows what's in his crystal ball for the future. *Matilda's* in his blood and he'll never leave but, for now,' she shrugged, 'he's the logical back up.'

'Kit's a qualified business man but he has itchy feet and travels for the property, and adventure.' Her cute mouth tipped into an indulgent grin. 'He's restless but loves to cut deals so I can see him helping with running the station but not living and working here permanently. Any woman that grabs his eye will have to be nomadic like him,' she chuckled.

Darcy was happy for the girl to chatter on. Her Beaumont blue eyes sparkled as she talked, wavy blonde hair cropped at her shoulders floating around her pixie face as she gestured and moved. She had perfect teeth and a big smile. Ed and Nina must have felt truly blessed when she came along after three sons.

'And me?' Elise added, spreading her arms wide. 'I'm a country girl. My heart's here and when the time's right, I'll be looking for a man in blue jeans not a suit. Just not any time soon.'

Another sweep of headlights and a vehicle approaching caught their attention and halted conversation.

'That'll be Mum and Dad,' Elise said unnecessarily, rising from her chair to meet them.

Murmured and questioning voices issued from the hallway for a while then all three entered the kitchen. Darcy rose and turned to see the emotional agony etched across their faces. Nina stood on tiptoe and reached out to hug her amid a profuse buzz of apologies.

Ed scowled. 'We're so sorry, Darcy.'

'Thanks. It was frightening,' was all she could say for now.

Ed looked in on the miserable image of his oldest son slumped askew on the sofa, snoring.

Darcy knew once the drink got you, you were in big trouble. She'd seen plenty of it up in the Territory. The despair, hard life or bad years, got you down and you couldn't get up. In her opinion, Hart might have been born into this life but he would never be a man of the land. She sensed the family already knew that but appeared to be clinging on to some hollow glimmer of hope.

Once everyone all held strong mugs of restorative coffee and settled around the table, Elise produced a tin of biscuits from the pantry.

'Will you press charges?' Ed tactfully probed Darcy.

Like Nina, he looked exhausted and gutted. Families everywhere went through tough stuff but, even grown, your kids were your kids for life and Darcy knew the Beaumonts would be there for their eldest troubled son. Although she was sure tonight's attack was a wakeup call for them.

'I'm prepared to put on my big girl boots and walk away,' Darcy conceded, 'but only if he's made accountable and you take action.'

'Appreciate it. We know it. Promise.' He glanced across to his wife, stonily silent nursing her hot drink, stoic but devastated. 'I believe our decision has been made for us.'

Nina nodded in agreement. Ed reached out across the table and they grasped hands. A body couldn't help but be touched by the heartfelt gesture. Darcy could see that reassessing the station's future from its traditional course was tough and heartbreaking. But with true outback steel this couple would weather these trials as their ancestors had done before them. Every generation faced its challenges.

It was growing late and Darcy, weak from her struggle with Hartley, tried to muster the physical strength and motivation to take her leave, get back on her bike and return to camp. Hartley seemed under control for now and the family would need to talk.

She was about to broach a goodbye and ride off into the night, furious to have been a victim of the cruel side of Hartley's nature but even more disappointed to have missed Mitch when the sound of yet another vehicle motor and its beam of headlights drifted into the homestead.

Ed frowned at Nina. 'Mitch say he was returning tonight?'

She shook her head. 'Haven't heard from him in two days.'

The vehicle door slammed, heavy clumping boots climbed the steps and crossed the veranda. Two clattering thuds told them they had been removed at the front door. There was a low growl from the dogs followed by a familiar male voice greeting them. The wire screen door whined open and slammed shut.

Softer long strides issued down the hallway until Mitch appeared in the kitchen doorway. Everyone turned or looked up at his arrival. His gaze of surprise whipped around the kitchen covering his parents, who he would have expected to see, but not Elise or Darcy, whose heart tripped over at the sight of him.

'Evening all. Hey sis.' He bent down to kiss her. 'Didn't know you were coming home.' She rose and embraced him in a warm sisterly hug.

'Darcy. Lovely surprise,' he said softly, leaning closer to kiss her cheek. The intimate gesture seemed to surprise the family but her cool response had him scowling.

'Saw Hart's truck outside. He here?' Mitch glanced around among everyone.

Ed took the reins, rose and nodded to the living room. 'In there. Drunk.'

Mitch peered around the corner then clearly sensing unease in the room, asked, 'Okay, so what's going on?'

'Come into the study, son, and I'll explain.' Ed led him away. With a quick backward glance and a frown, he followed his father.

What felt to Darcy like a long ten minutes later, father and son returned. One glance at Mitch revealed a restrained seething anger, his whole body rigid, as if poised for action. If Hartley had been awake and sober, Darcy guessed he would have punched his brother out for her. Then, worse, and with agonising softness he looked down at her and the depth of his sorrow and protection in his eyes tore her apart.

Heedless of the family around watching she reached out to grasp his hand. 'I'll be fine,' she whispered, fighting back tears. 'Please, sit down.'

She had only ever seen the strength, humour and warmth of a country boy's nature and heart in this man. Never this barely withheld rage.

His mouth thinned. 'Something *will* be done. Enough,' he growled through gritted teeth.

To no one in particular, Darcy said, 'I should get back to camp,' and slowly rose to her feet.

Mitch was beside her in an instant. 'You're staying here.'

'All due respect,' she muttered wearily, 'but under the same roof as your brother? I don't think so.' Receiving his hurtful glance, Darcy could see her challenge to his offer cut deep.

His jaw ground, he planted two strong hands on his hips and looked her straight in the eye. 'Fair enough. I'll bring my swag and sleep close.'

Darcy was nothing short of deeply touched but she shook her head. 'There's really no need. You should be here with your family.'

He shot a heavy loaded glance that stood no argument. 'I insist.'

Darcy shrugged dismissively. 'Your call.'

She tried to sound easy about his suggestion but liked the firm way Mitch made her feel like she was being taken care of. Despite outback women learning early how to do that for themselves, Mitch's protectiveness warmed the deepest corners of her heart.

Despite the evening's sickening events and perceptible strain among them, it still seemed the most natural thing in the world for her to hug Ed, Nina and Elise before she left. Mitch's parents again murmured their apologies which Darcy casually dismissed. Elise trotted after them down the hallway to the front door.

'I'll meet you at camp,' Darcy turned to Mitch as she descended the front steps and headed for her bike.

'Don't leave until I'm in my ute right behind you,' he scowled, tugging on his boots under the veranda.

'Okay,' she said meekly, surprised by the depth of his concern and strong command.

As she donned her helmet, she heard his modulated conversation with Elise.

'What brought you home, sis?'

'You know me,' she sighed. 'This place is a magnet. I love it.'

'Unlike our big brother,' he muttered.

'Let it go, Mitch.' From the corner of her eye as she buckled her helmet strap, Darcy saw Elise put a hand on his arm. 'Actually,' she continued, 'it's for a photographic university project I'm using as a private portfolio. Any excuse to get out here,' she chuckled.

Darcy caught Mitch's indulgent brotherly smile. 'Sounds like someone else I know.'

Elise lowered her voice but she still overheard. 'Darcy maybe?'

'Don't be cheeky,' Mitch snapped a glance in her direction.

Darcy quickly looked away pretending ignorance.

'You're usually a straight shooter. Why so coy?' his sister continued to tease. 'Some truth in what I said, huh?'

Mitch kissed Elise on the cheek. 'Catch you in the morning. Probably need a family conference. Keep an eye on Hart.'

'Sure.' She waved him off and returned indoors.

When Mitch reached Darcy, he hovered beside her as she sat astride her bike. 'Are you sure you're okay?'

She nodded and pressed the starter button. 'It's getting late.' She raised her voice over the idling engine. 'Let's go.'

With his ute headlights trained on her close behind and lighting up the track ahead, Darcy and Mitch returned to her camp. She watched in amazement as he carried his swag over from the ute and set it up right in front of her tent flap door. She could not have felt more cherished and secure. How could two brothers be so different?

Darcy tried to settle for the night inside her tent snug in her sleeping bag despite the late winter chill. Annoyingly, she found herself restless and wakeful. Not only from her scare with Hartley who had threatened her life and left her shaken. There was also the pleasantly disturbing awareness of Mitch sleeping so close. Like, just through a stretch of canvas close.

When she grew exasperated, fed up with tossing, turning and staring at the tent roof above, she pushed back the covers, pulled on a jumper over the jeans and shirt she had been too tired to bother changing before bed and crawled to the door. As she pushed aside the door flap, wondering how she could step over Mitch without waking him, she discovered there was no need for concern.

He was sitting up by the fire, stoking it, wide awake too.

He didn't even turn around. 'Can't sleep either?'

'No,' she groaned, ruffling her hair to tidy it a little.

'Not surprised. You have good reason.' He patted the ground beside him. 'Join me?'

Darcy settled beside him their bodies aligned and touching, the glowing coals rekindled and warming flames licking around the logs Mitch had added to the fire.

He nudged her shoulder. 'Hungry? These coals would make great toast.'

She shook her head, despite realising she had missed dinner tonight. The constant buzzing question, one of many that had kept her awake, still circled her mind. Should she have stayed at camp and avoided the homestead drama? Ironically, Mitch returned tonight and probably would have come out here anyway so there was no need for her trip back to the house.

'I know you *said* you're okay but do you want to talk about it?'

Darcy shrugged. In the firelight's glow he placed a comforting hand on her knee, drawing her closer.

'Dad gave me a run down but you have no idea how-'

''Don't. It's okay,' she interrupted his distress, wrapping both arms around the nearest one of his and snuggling against his warm muscled body. Darcy stared into the fire shaking her head in wonder, her voice lowered. 'It's over. Boy, Elise is a fireball. I was so relieved when she arrived. Of course she knows him well and gave him heaps. With both barrels.'

'Our brother's collecting a poor reputation. But he's a grown man and there comes a time when you need to call a stop and start taking responsibility for your actions.'

'It's so sad for your family. I'm sorry.'

'We've all kept up the hope that Hartley would one day want to be part of *Matilda Downs* again but that won't happen.'

'No. Not after his outburst tonight.' She hesitated. 'His assault was a threat. A warning because I know he's definitely involved now with the Professor.'

'Because you saw them together in town?' Mitch's shadowed face puckered into a frown. 'I didn't think he saw us that night?'

Darcy shook her head. 'He didn't. I saw him again. The other night after we changed my bike tyres, I took the bike for a spin. Into town. I prowled around for a while. I saw the Professor and another man leave town so I followed them out to the turn off into the jump up. They met Hart out there.'

'You went out alone in the dark knowing they were suss?' he turned to her and growled.

'I hid and I swear no one saw me while I was there or they would have nabbed me quick sticks. Hartley saw me leaving. He told me tonight. I thought I got away clean.'

'Don't ever put yourself in danger like that again. Hell, Darcy, you're a magnet for trouble,' he muttered.

'Well I have my bodyguard here now,' she teased.

Mitch mellowed. 'Okay, so what happened out at the jump up?'

'Hartley was already there when Stirling and another guy arrived. Sounded like his name was either Bennie or Bernie. I got their four wheel drive number plate.'

Darcy scrambled to her feet and tore out the page from her notebook in her backpack in the tent. As she handed it to Mitch and sat down again, she said, 'That should identify him.'

'I'll get a mate to check it out.'

'In the local police?'

'No, a lawyer friend. I'll tell you more about him later. I can't believe my brother has turned to crime.'

'It's all about the money. He said so tonight.'

'I'm surprised but he's always craved a life away from farming.'

'After the men met the other night out at the jump up, they disappeared down a narrow canyon and into a cave. I couldn't follow. There was no cover. But they probably intend to use it as a temporary stockpile.'

'Could you find it again in daylight?'

Darcy nodded. 'Pretty sure. Wasn't that far out of town. Maybe ten or fifteen minutes then north on a track into the jump up.'

'Right.' Mitch folded the piece of paper and tucked it into his shirt pocket. 'I'll text Glenn about the number plate tonight so he can get onto it first thing in the morning. He has…contacts.'

'The gang is planning something that's for sure and it looks like Stirling's paying for local help. Hartley and this older guy, Bennie, or whoever.'

Mitch frowned. 'Trying to think of someone in the district by that name who needs money.'

'The Professor keeps getting away with it but after the other night's bush meeting, this is shaping up like his usual jobs. Same mysterious movements and happenings. Whatever they're planning, it's big and it's soon. I'd love to know the bigger fry behind him.'

'Frankly,' Darcy turned aside to Mitch, resting her chin on his arm, their faces close, 'I fear for our fossil find over there.' She nodded toward the dig site and crew camp. 'Maybe they're waiting until we get him out of the ground.

We've done one side of him in plaster and he's ready to roll over to do the other one. He's huge but he'll be totally vulnerable then. And moveable. But he's going to need some heavy equipment.

'I've asked the local dinosaur museum for help and they've offered it. *Mitch* may end up in their complex, depending what you decide. They're fully set up for it and it makes sense to keep him local.' She paused. 'We'll most likely want to return here over the coming winters for future digs. It's a substantial site with massive potential.'

'That mean you're returning?'

Darcy softened her voice. '*Matilda Downs* has lots to offer.'

'I think so,' he chuckled. 'What you're uncovering sounds incredible. I'll see how the land lies in the morning at the homestead but I'd love to come back and take a look. Haven't had a chance in recent days. My apologies for neglecting you so that you've needed to take a back seat.'

'I'm not needy but I've…missed having you around.' After a thoughtful pause, she added, 'These have been the most rewarding and fulfilling weeks of my life. In every way. Professionally and personally.'

'I found a little outback gold and sunshine myself.' He leaned closer to steal a soft slow kiss.

Darcy sighed while their lips still touched.

'That one was a taster. This is for real.' Mitch pushed his hands up into her hair, drew her tight against him and performed miracles with his mouth that left Darcy gasping with need. 'After what happened earlier,' he murmured, 'it's not really the best night for you to take this further.'

'I am still anxious,' she admitted, 'but you're helping settle me right down. So don't stop,' she whispered. 'I need more soothing.'

Mitch obliged. They sank back onto the cool grass together and he continued his own personal brand of healing.

Later, after they had explored each other and finally broke apart, Mitch said, 'I have news of my own.'

'Mmm?' Darcy was still bathing in the glow of Mitch's therapy, her mind in pleasured neutral and the sure-fire likelihood Mitch would want to complete what they had started here tonight after the dig ended and life's current upheavals had settled down.

'I found Bima,' he said quietly.

Chapter 11

Darcy sat bolt upright and straightened her clothes, instantly knowing who Mitch referred to when he mentioned Bima. 'The university cleaner? How do you even know about him and why were you looking?'

Mitch sat up beside her, plucking off blades of grass caught in her hair. He reached for her hand and squeezed it. 'It tore me up watching you suffer. I wanted to see what I could do to help. Got my lawyer mate, Glenn, on board and he blitzed red tape. I hope you don't mind but we checked out the details of the investigation and court hearing when you went after Stirling.'

Darcy frowned. 'That's all in Darwin.'

He nodded. 'Glenn wanted to see all the evidence. Find out what was missed maybe.'

'You went to the Territory? That's why you were away?'

'I didn't tell you and raise your hopes in case

it all came to nothing.'

In the fire's orange glow, Mitch hesitated, his face taking on a humble bashfulness, his self-conscious manner suggesting a reluctance to admit the depth of his efforts to help, already revealed by the feelings he had shown her tonight.

Darcy was blown away that he would secretly and with utter unselfish initiative do this for her. 'That was a mighty fine gesture Mr. Beaumont,' she said softly.

Mitch's roaming gaze all over her from those absorbing blue eyes only confirmed what they had just shared together. They hadn't fully made love but had certainly explored each other with passion.

'I'd pretty much do anything for you, Doc.' The words any woman yearned to hear, especially if you were falling for the guy. 'We men do flip a second look or buckle at the knees sometimes when females are around.'

Darcy scoffed. 'You wouldn't be one of those.'

'I've been known to weaken.'

'No! Big strong man like you?'

'Hard to stay focused around you, Darcy. You're not like any other woman I've met.'

'Ah now, that was your first mistake. Assuming I was going to be like them.'

She jabbed him in the ribs deeply affected in the richest way by what he had just confided. 'Better tell me what you've found.'

'My pleasure.'

Darcy listened to the deep low tones of Mitch's voice as he recounted his approach to his lawyer mate in Brisbane, Glenn's inside help and the reason for their productive trip to Darwin.

'You went through all the files and hearing papers?'

'Yep. I was helping Glenn search for anything that looked suspicious or didn't add up. Then he found a clue. Bima made a damaging statement but for whatever reason it was never presented as evidence. Because the police lacked solid evidence in their investigation it appears they didn't pursue or challenge it.'

'I knew Bima was questioned,' Darcy said. 'When he disappeared before the hearing, I have to tell you I was more than a little suspicious and afraid for his wellbeing and safety. Way too much of a coincidence.'

'Apparently they tried intimidation. Broke into his flat so he fled back home to Indonesia. They didn't chase him. Out of the way and scared, I guess they figured he wouldn't pose a threat. I'm surprised after what you've told me about Stirling and his methods that Bima's statement didn't quietly disappear. It was still in the file, just never used. So Glenn suggested we follow up Bima's Indonesian address. He had to return to his office but I jumped on a plane to see if I could find him.'

'To Indonesia?' Darcy gaped.

'Yep. Amazingly he was at the same address in the same little house living with his mother and wife and three young children. Once I proved my association with you, talked to him and gained his confidence, he let me tape the conversation and I showed him a copy of his statement which he verified. He agreed to give evidence against Stirling if he's ever caught and brought to justice.'

'Wow, that's unbelievable. That little man sure has guts.'

'There was something else very interesting in Bima's statement. Stirling often sent him out to clean his yacht at the marina in Cullen Bay.'

Darcy frowned. 'That was beyond his university duties.'

Mitch shrugged. 'Sure was but he needed the money to send back home. So he did the job, got paid extra and kept quiet. Said he was only sent out to the boat after it had returned from a trip out to sea.'

'Do you think the yacht is a clue?'

'Can't rule it out.'

'But I only ever saw Stirling and his friends on it in the marina having parties. And sometimes they loaded it up with fishing gear and headed out. Except as I said before, I never saw the Professor go aboard for those trips.'

'Are you sure they were loading fishing gear?' Mitch queried slowly.

Darcy groaned. 'Oh, no. Don't tell me-'

'They may have been smuggling out you-know-what.'

'Damn,' she cursed softly.

'It's a big isolated place out at sea. Lot of unpatrolled coastline. Border Protection can't be everywhere.'

Darcy shook her head. 'Stirling or his superiors would never risk being seen close to shore. They're big time. They wouldn't want their operations uncovered.'

'I agree. I've been Googling and researching. Three nautical miles off shore forms part of coastal waters. Between twelve and twenty four miles out to sea, patrols can still take action. But,' Mitch paused for effect, grinning, 'beyond that out on the high seas it's international waters outside a country's territorial shoreline. No state has sovereignty or controls it. Everyone has freedom of fishing, navigation, overflight, that kind of thing.'

'Wow,' Darcy chuckled, impressed, 'for an outback sheep farmer you're right up with things, aren't you?'

'No excuse for ignorance these days,' Mitch beamed, suppressing his secret pride.

In the brief seconds of silence that fell between them, Darcy knew a light bulb moment. 'Holy shit.' She pushed out a deep breath. 'His boat must be the link.'

'It's our best one yet.'

She scoffed at herself in frustration. 'And I'll

bet all this time he was loading fossils *not* fishing gear right under my nose.' She raised her knees and sank her head into her hands.

Mitch's big arm went around her. 'At least we've possibly cracked how he smuggles the spoils out of the country. We just need to work out how he gets the stuff to the yacht and where it's offloaded.'

'Simple.'

After that, they boiled the billy, heedless of the early morning hours, and drank mugs of tea playing *what ifs* for hours. Getting fossils from land to sea. Where at sea they transferred their goods. From the small boat to a bigger ship? If a chopper or sea plane might also be involved. Whichever way they analysed it, seriously big money was behind it all.

And the sixty-four thousand dollar question. Out in all that ocean, exactly where did all this take place?

'But Stirling's never on board his yacht you say?' Mitch rose, stretched and added another log to the fire. Darcy nodded. 'But you've kept diaries of his movements?'

'Yes. As much as I could gather.' She grew excited, knowing where his thoughts were headed. 'But that's all in Brisbane under lock and key.'

'Maybe when you get back, you could go over them and we'll try to match up the yacht departure dates from the marina in Darwin with his trips to Bali. I have a hunch they'll coincide.'

Darcy studied Mitch with passion and amazement. 'If you hadn't found those fossils and contacted the museum and I hadn't met you none of this would have come to light. At least not so soon.'

'Team work,' Mitch said and they high-fived.

'So what's next?'

'Nothing much more we can do on the fossil front. How you holding up? Weary yet?'

'I'm too wired to sleep. How about you?'

'I can keep going a while longer.'

'Guess we can sleep when we're extinct,' she quipped.

Mitch groaned at her corny joke. A comfortable silence settled between them but Darcy sensed something on his mind so she waited, knowing he would spit it out when he was ready.

Finally he said, 'What are your plans about Hart's aggression tonight?'

Darcy knew the issue would be addressed between them eventually. It was Mitch's brother and a serious offence.

She shrugged easily. 'That's a big part of why I couldn't sleep. I could seek legal advice, press charges,' she spoke quietly as if almost to herself, staring into the fire. Going over yet again every possible scenario in her mind. 'I don't want my tussle with Hartley to be dismissed as unimportant or without consequences.'

'Absolutely not. You're a victim of trauma and my whole family fully appreciate your rights and will support your stand. Whatever you decide we'll understand.'

'That's the problem. I can't decide. There's so much involved and at stake here. But there are options. If Hartley will go for it, there could be a solution for everyone. Bottom line is I don't want to cause scandal for your family but its clear something's weighing heavily on Hartley's mind and he needs help. But he also needs to atone for what he did to me.'

With his hands on his knees, Mitch sighed and pushed his hands through his thick sandy hair. 'I swear,' he said strongly, 'he never used to be like this. A little wild maybe but something's happened to tip him over the edge this year.'

'I hope everything turns out okay for him,' Darcy said, 'but first hear me out. What about if you talk to him. Try and find out why he's so desperate for money. You know, even while he was playing mean tonight, there was fear in his eyes as much as bravado. Could have been because I wouldn't cooperate. If he won't confide for whatever reason, tell him there's a way out for him to make amends and break free from this mess.'

Mitch raised his eyebrows with interest. 'What do you have in mind?'

'That we can do something for him if he does something for us.'

'Sounds intriguing. I'm listening.'

'It's a long shot based on how little I know him, and it should probably come from you, but how about you tell him I won't take any legal action if he agrees to help us gather information on Stirling?'

'You mean for him to stay in the operation and double-cross them?' Mitch slowly shook his head. 'It's an ideal solution but I seriously doubt he'd consider that. And it could be way too risky.'

'Not if he's careful and acts himself like he's always done. He's an insider. He could tell us when and where their next move is. When we have enough information we could approach the police.'

'That would put Hart in danger.'

'Not if Hartley kept Stirling's trust. Continued his loyalty. That's when we could go to the law and tell them whatever Hartley gives us for their next job. We might even find out why he wants money so badly,' she maintained. 'Maybe it's not the reason he says.'

'Dicey odds, Darcy,' he sighed, 'but as you says it's a chance for him to right a wrong. Maybe more than one.'

'If the authorities know Hartley is cooperating to help, maybe they will cut a deal with him. Lessen any conviction or sentence because he's involved. What about your lawyer mate? Could he advise us?'

Mitch nodded. 'It's all feasible. In theory.' He paused. 'Okay. When I call Glenn about the number plate I'll lay it all out. Get his opinion. Might take a day or two though. We'll have to be patient. Glenn's a stress junkie. Thrives on it. Don't want to push his friendship but I'm sure he'll help where he can.' Mitch entwined his fingers with Darcy. 'That's a damned fine suggestion and generous of you. If it all comes to something, the family will be hugely grateful.'

'And what about you, Mitch? How do you plan to show *your* gratitude?' Darcy murmured a sultry appeal.

'I'm absolutely sure I'll think of something,' he drawled.

'Good.' Darcy yawned.

'You better get some sleep, huh?'

'Or I'll be dozing down in the dig pit tomorrow alongside *Mitch,* you mean?' she chuckled, bemused with exhaustion. 'Wanna join me in my sleeping bag?'

'Won't be much room for either of us.'

'That's the idea,' she whispered, grinning.

'And you won't get a wink of the sleep you desperately need.'

'Why not?'

'Because I would be keeping you awake,' Mitch growled, pulling Darcy to her feet and pressing a warm tender kiss to her forehead, as sexy as if it had been on the mouth.

'Damn. You're refusing me?'

'Not refusing. Postponing. And I can assure you now, Doc, it will be worth the wait. For both of us.'

Darcy woke to the usual melodic chorus of bush and water birds chortling outside her tent high up in the coolabah trees or flapping in the waterhole nearby. The world was waking.

She stretched, blessed with a deep contentment she hadn't felt in way too long. Last night's memories of many hours with Mitch were like a restorative for her soul. Mitch was right outside her unzipped door flap. She had left it open in case he changed his mind. Although she doubted a stretch of canvas would stop him if he put his mind to it.

But when she scrambled outside it was to see him wide awake, his swag already rolled up, his arms full of collected firewood. Flames already licking beneath her blackened billy singing itself to the boil.

When he caught sight of her, he beamed and her heart skipped. 'Good morning.'

'Didn't you sleep?'

'Grabbed a few hours. Like to head back to the homestead. See how the family's doing.'

'Of course.' Darcy folded her arms and yawned. 'Thanks for my healthy wood pile.'

He tossed his swag into the back of his ute, stepped closer and said, 'You're welcome,' just before folding a hand beneath her chin to tilt up her face and accept his kiss.

It was warm and lingering, sparking every one of her sleepy senses into life.

'You're ridiculously adorable first thing in the morning,' he drawled.

Darcy's heart flipped again. 'Until my first mug of tea this is as good as it gets. See you later,' she murmured.

As he waved and strode away, she felt deprived but clung to the knowledge that he would be back.

Chapter 12

A brisk solar shower soon livened Darcy up, followed by one of Dawnie's hearty breakfasts. Doubly appreciated this morning because she had missed dinner last night.

Then it was everyone down to the dig pit where two of the women on hands and knees alongside Darcy proceeded to finish digging through underneath *Mitch*, carefully excavating around the edges to isolate him.

By mid-morning, the fossil was finally free from the ground and with the men helping too, their major find was laboriously rolled over so Darcy and her fellow diggers could coat his underside in its plastic jacket until the entire specimen was safely encased in a hard shell for the trip back to the museum.

Because it made logistical sense as the true size of their find became apparent, Darcy had already discussed and arranged to store their immense covered skeleton at the huge local museum complex in Winton. To which they naturally and enthusiastically agreed with much excitement. They knew about the dig and Darcy updated them on what was being unearthed.

Her real life Mitch hadn't reappeared by lunch so, together with the digging crew, boosted by the elation of their successes, everyone ate a noisy meal amid lively chatter in the catering tent.

Afterwards, they all donned sunhats and gloves again, the team returning to the dig, Darcy to her tent to catch up with labelling and making detailed notes of where each specimen was found. Along with other relevant information, she sealed each one in a plastic bag, writing labels on the outside.

She re-joined the crew on site again later to find them standing and stretching taking a well-deserved break. Helen beamed down indulgently on *Mitch* and their other bigger pieces also being put into their plaster jackets as though they were all her own children. Darcy chuckled in amusement.

'What?' Helen grunted in her usual forthright good natured way. 'You're never too old for dinosaurs. Hell this guy is way older than me and he's still looking good.'

Their laughter burst into an echo across the open plains like the territorial chuckling call of kookaburras often heard out here in the bush.

Standing looking down over their weeks of labour they stared, pointed and marvelled.

Everyone among them dusty, sore and dishevelled would leave with wonderful memories of fantastic discoveries, even the smallest one like an exciting strike of gold. Just before lunch, Marg had scratched out what Darcy identified as a tibia and Murray standing over his usual tireless place at the screening table had separated a tooth tip.

Even at this late stage, the diggers were weary but happily so, and still thrilled by each little treasure they found.

Afternoon smoko had just been called and they straggled over to the food tent when Mitch finally arrived back. As he left the ute and strolled toward her, Darcy spread her arms wide to encompass the entire dig site, a broad smile on her suntanned face.

'We found all this because you and your quad bike stumbled over those skull fragments.'

Mitch stood beside her, feet astride, hands on his Wrangler-clad hips, his squinting gaze drifting over the excavated landscape. 'Amazing. Sorry I couldn't get out more often to help.'

'There's been a lot going on around here.'

'Spent the morning doing some digging of my own.' They sat on the edge of the metre deep pit hollow, their legs dangling over the side. 'That's why I was late getting back out here.' Mitch didn't make her wait for news but got right into it. 'Got the number plate identified on that white four wheel drive. It's old Bernie Woods from *Mulga Plains*, about two hours north west of the highway. Once I had that information, I confronted Hart.'

'How did he pull up this morning?'

'Seedy but sane. Family kept him in the homestead last night for obvious reasons. We laid all the facts on the table. Put on some pressure and he cracked on the low down about Bernie's situation. Turns out the old guy's cattle station is run down. Sounds like his property is going under. He'll be needing money.'

Darcy shook her head and scoffed. 'Ripe for Stirling to pick him off. Told you the man does his homework. Only uses the most vulnerable to manipulate.'

'Woods keeps to himself. Wife left him years ago. Not sure about any kids. Employs a few aboriginal stockmen who stick by him.'

'A sad situation. Life is tough out here.'

'Hart said Bernie can't manage it anymore and it's got on top of him. So once the old man's identity was established, Dad told Hart he would pay out his share of *Matilda Downs* if he wanted to start a new life somewhere else. Not sure if it was in appreciation or irony that the money he was so desperate for had just been offered but it's probably the first time I've ever seen my big brother cry. Mum kept the jug boiled and Elise worked on Hart. She's pretty blunt but she's always known that's the best way to approach him. All these years, the folks have been too soft. Talk about fate.' Mitch shook his head. 'Our little sister deciding to come home last night and rescuing you and today, the culprit in all this finally opening up.'

'He did?' Darcy eagerly listened.

'I started by pointing out his rough handling of you. Explained how important you are to me.'

'I am?' she teased, nudging his shoulder.

'You know it,' he drawled. 'Then I detailed exactly what I might have done to him if he'd harmed you in the slightest way.'

'I do have a spread of bruises.'

'Damn, Darcy, I'm so sorry.'

'They'll heal. Go on.'

'According to Glenn,' he said, 'assault causing harm carries up to a seven year gaol term. Hart got edgy when we told him the potential sentence for his crime. I laid out your offer. Said you'd consider forgetting any charges if he agreed to help. And Elise being a witness, you'd have a strong case. Outlined what you suggested last night. Tried to warn him about Stirling. Got him thinking.

'After that there was lots of pacing and arguing. When Hart started being more reasonable and approachable, Dad asked him why he needed the money. Why he didn't ask family first. Come to them for help. Took him a while but Hart eventually spilt out his heart.'

'Too often men think they need to be tough,'

Darcy said, 'and don't see the need to tell anyone how they're really feeling. That they're not doing okay.'

'When Hart first broke down I didn't know whether to be disgusted that he was weak or proud and supportive that he had the guts to come clean.' As Mitch continued, Darcy could see he was deeply affected by his brother's revelations. 'Then I realised he'd locked up a lifetime of emotional pain. I thought he was weak losing his temper when he was just feeling frustrated and cornered. Man do I feel bad for judging my own brother so harsh.'

'It's called being human,' Darcy murmured. 'We don't always get things right.'

'Yeah. So, bottom line with Hart, deep down of course it was his damn pride keeping him mean and isolated from the family. But also a lifetime of being hounded, especially when he was just a kid by Grandpa Eli that *Matilda Downs* was his responsibility one day.'

'At that age, we're so impressionable.'

'So he crushed his guilt that he wasn't interested yet he suffered an obligation to do his duty and what was expected of every oldest Beaumont son. That's why he raged against it growing up.' Mitch reflected for a moment. 'One thing that used to ease his mind was his guitar. Just sitting strumming it. Not often. It was a go-to when he was desperate.'

'Music in Hart's soul?' Darcy marvelled.

'Hard to imagine from my encounters with him.'

'You've seen him at his lowest,' Mitch pointed out, 'and he hasn't played the guitar in years. At least I haven't heard him. Maybe that was part of the problem. He distanced himself from family and gave up doing the one thing that gave him some sort of peace. I tell you, Darcy, you wouldn't believe it after last night's outburst from him but Hart's a broken man.'

She looked across at Mitch and saw him swallow hard against his emotions.

'You won't believe what else came to light. You were right. Stirling knows how to get to people where it hurts the most. Even my big brother, tough as he tried to be, crumbled when the Professor threatened his family.'

'Family!' Darcy's gasped. 'What, secretly married or something?' she said in jest but when Mitch slowly turned to look at her and hold her surprised gaze, she added, 'No way!'

'Close. Loves a little thing ten years younger and she's pregnant. He buckled under Stirling's pressure thinking he was protecting them. Was going to use the promised money for a new life with her.'

'Well I'll be damned. How did Hart meet her?'

'At one of the pubs in town. She was behind the bar. Backpacker. English. Name of Rose. I seem to remember her.' His forehead crinkled into a thoughtful frown. 'Sweet girl actually.

Curly blonde hair with a charming accent.'

'Where is Rose now?'

'In Winton but it's a catch 22. She doesn't want to leave Hart and he doesn't want her to go but neither of them wants to stay out here. They were banking on Stirling's money.'

'Is Rose safe? She's not being threatened?' Mitch's hesitation to reply alarmed her and told her to start worrying. 'He's not!'

'Stirling won't let the girl leave town until this latest job is done.'

'You couldn't get her away? Say, out here to the homestead?' Darcy suggested. 'She'd still be in the district. Hart could plead something about her pregnancy. Claim she needs to be careful. Can't be on her own.'

Mitch frowned. 'Possible. Need to think on that one. She's the reason Hart's been missing so much. Being afraid for her just made him meaner and more desperate but once everything came out this morning, Hart calmed down. A problem shared, you know?' he shrugged. 'In the end he said if we helped him protect Rose, he'd agree to help us get Stirling.'

Darcy clamped both hands over her face. 'What? Oh my God, that's awesome.' She blinked back tears of emotion and disbelief. 'That's a damn decent trade-off for his behaviour last night.'

'His drunken bout just proved he was growing hopeless. Getting Rose out here to the homestead might be difficult but keeping her safe without endangering her or my parents could prove tricky. Elise said she'd stick around longer.'

'How did your family take all this amazing news?'

'Ecstatic actually. Means that Hart might actually settle down now and they have that grandchild to look forward to that they've always wanted. Takes the pressure off the rest of us,' he grinned, then his face clouded, 'but we're not clear of the mulga yet.'

'No. You need to get Rose to safety somehow first without making Stirling suspicious. Preferably tonight or first thing tomorrow. Before we move *Mitch* and Stirling finds out. Because I'll tell you what else has me worried. If he's planning an operation soon, it means he has something in mind to steal. If our big guy is his target, I want *Mitch* safe and secure in the Winton dinosaur museum fast. Then I'll double the watch and security on site here until we're finished in a few days.'

'Okay. I'll leave you to organise your man down there in the pit and I'll see what we can do for Rose.'

Mitch scrambled to his feet, helped Darcy up then hugged and kissed her. She was just bathing in the effects of their heady moments of passion when she noticed the crew all dawdling back from smoko.

As Mitch strode for the ute, waved to everyone and drove away, Helen sidled closer. 'You're spending a lot of time with that outback stud.'

Darcy grinned to herself. 'You keep your eyes off my man.' Although bursting with happiness at what possibly lay ahead in her future she also remained deeply anxious about the immediate days to come.

Helen wiggled her eyebrows and nudged Darcy. 'Gotta say you two do look good together. Didn't take him long to stretch his feet out in front of your camp fire, huh?' she chuckled.

'For which I'll be forever grateful. Now,' Darcy turned back to the dig pit, 'pressure has just risen a notch. We need to get that big guy out of here. While I make some calls to get manpower and stuff happening with the museum, can you round up the men? Alert them we're going to need lots of muscle, equipment, all the pallets crated and loaded with everything we've found so far and that front end digger over there ready to go. Be too late to organise anything today, so I'd guess in the morning.'

As word spread around the camp, the dig team sensed Darcy's urgency and everyone cooperated, each feeling their own kinship to the new sauropod nature had exposed for them and they had all helped extract from earth's grasp.

As Mitch sped along the dirt track toward the homestead, dust billowing out behind his ute and the lowering sun making a golden backdrop to the homestead, Hart's black truck was still parked out front. Good. He either hadn't wanted to leave or the folks didn't let him.

After this morning's family discussion and his big brother's breakdown, he was encouraged that if Hart played his cards right the future was looking much more positive for him than it had in a long time. He felt like he was getting back the older daredevil brother he knew as a kid.

But they had to help get this fossil smuggling mess sorted for Darcy first. Which ironically now involved his brother.

He leapt up the front steps, pushed off his boots to thump on the veranda and went inside. The aromas of his mother's renowned country cooking drew him down the hallway into the kitchen.

She smiled as he entered. 'Lamb casserole and chocolate pudding. Elise is working on her photo project in the office and the men,' she nodded toward the adjoining living room through the half closed French doors, 'are still talking.'

'That's what they were doing when I left,' he chided.

Nina gave her son a cautious glance. 'Heard Hart's mobile ring just a moment ago.'

Mitch joined his father and brother. He could

have murdered a beer but his mother, wise woman under the circumstances, must have raided the lemon tree because he noted the tall jug of homemade lemonade on the centre table instead of alcohol and poured himself a glass.

'What's happening?' he asked as he sat down.

Hart looked fresher and had changed his day old crumpled clothes for a clean white shirt and black jeans. Probably ducked across to his cottage and taken a shower. Mitch was pleased to see a return of that smart pride in himself. Suggested a positive edge to his thinking. Help haul him from the worst of that nasty desperation he'd seen in him last night.

'Stirling phoned. Been waiting for his call.' Hart sat forward, hands clenched between his knees. 'Wants a meeting ASAP. Told him I'd need an hour to get into town. He doesn't want to be seen so we fixed it for seven tonight south of town.'

Out of instinct all men checked their watches. Two hours.

'Right. As you know, I've just been out to update Darcy. Since it looks like Stirling's job is going down soon, she suggested we get Rose to safety out here beforehand. On the drive back to the homestead I hatched a plan. We need to get our timing right. So how about ten minutes after seven, Rose phones you and says she's sick, needs medical help or whatever. You'll need to keep him talking at your meeting until she calls.

'I'll head into town behind you at a distance. You meet Stirling, I'll go around to Rose, help her pack or whatever, grab her bags then disappear. After she calls, you scoot around to her flat, pick her up and take her to the hospital.'

'I've told her not to trust anybody right now,' Hart advised darkly. 'She'll need you to prove who you are.'

'Fair enough. Give you, me and Rose a password that only we will know. I'll drive around behind the hospital, she walks straight through and comes to me out the back then I bring her here. You wait around inside the hospital for a half hour or hour or so, then phone Stirling and tell him Rose is being kept in overnight and you're staying in her flat in town. You'll need to update us on what he plans next.'

Hart rubbed his hands along his jeans and rose, pacing. 'This better work. Anything happens to that girl…'

'It won't,' Mitch assured him. 'We're on your side, bro. Promise I'll guard her with my life.'

Not surprisingly, Mitch's thoughts turned to Darcy and he knew exactly how his brother was feeling right now.

Nina entered the room wringing a tea towel in her hands. 'Think I caught most of that conversation. So there's five for dinner including Rose and Hart's staying in town. Ed, how about you nip out to the waterhole and see if Darcy would like to come join us for dinner. By then,

Mitch might have some news from Hart about whatever is happening next.' She shrugged and slowly shook her head, the ghost of a confused smile on her face. 'I thought sheep were trouble enough. Now it's fossils.'

Mitch's heart warmed to its core to have his mother include Darcy in their family gathering. Didn't take a woman as smart as his mother to guess that the Doc was becoming an important person in his life. She wasn't showing it but he'd be willing to bet that two potential new women partners in her sons' lives and a baby on the way just within the past two weeks had put more than a spring in her step. Deep down, she was a hard worker and homemaker but she'd be loving every busy minute of it all.

While Ed headed out to Darcy's waterhole camp, in town Mitch headed for Rose's flat while his brother went to meet their adversary. He parked around the corner and walked to her door, keeping an eye out for any other cars or people around. As luck would have it, her street was quiet. Nothing looked suspicious so he hoped no one was on watch.

When he knocked on the front door, he took a deep breath, unsure what to expect. From his very first glance as the door squeaked open, he was reassured. He remembered the girl from the pub bar, prettier than he recalled, curly blonde hair playing just above her shoulders, and a sharp wariness behind those baby blue eyes. But in that job she'd worn a tight black tee shirt and short skirt.

This young woman standing before him now was nobody's fool. Sensibly dressed in cargoes, a loose tee shirt over a very slightly rounded stomach and sneakers.

Mitch extended a hand. *'Boomerang.'* He grinned as he gave the password.

Maybe the encouraging smile did it because she beamed, just short of laughing and said, 'You're obviously Mitch. I'm Rose. All packed.'

He followed her down a narrow hallway into a bedroom and pulled up short. 'That's it?' He eyed her one large soft overnight case.

'I've backpacked for years. I travel light.'

Mitch could see why Hart was smitten. Her sweet looks were deceptive. She could probably kill a snake with her bare hands. Just the kind of woman Hart needed. Quietly strong.

'Right. I'm out of here. You call Hart in,' he checked his watch, 'say, another five to seven minutes, and I'll meet you out back of the hospital.'

'Thanks,' she said softly, standing in the middle of the room looking momentarily lost, her composure floundering for just a moment, her eyes glistening with moisture.

Moved, Mitch said warmly, 'If you're going to be my sister-in-law, let's hug it out, okay?'

She laughed through her threatening tears, they hugged quickly then he left.

Chapter 13

Damn, Mitch thought, as he drove around the back streets of town to the hospital grounds. It was frustrating not being able to see or hear Hart's meeting with Stirling and that Rose's phone call had worked so Hart could bring her safely to hospital.

He figured he had about a fifteen minute wait, played country music on the radio to steady his nerves. This had to work. With Rose safe, it was down to Hart bringing them the information they needed to go to the authorities while at the same time keeping himself out of trouble with Stirling and not raising any suspicions that he was now playing both sides.

A fierce defence of his brother rose in him that he hadn't felt in years, detached as Hart had been from the family. Mitch softly cursed at the waste of years. But they were all on the same page again both individually and as a family, and all had each other's back.

Incredibly, it seemed he and Hart had their romantic lives sorted. Spirited Elise was bound to enter and spice up some man's life someday. While according to their rover brother Kit, he was always on the lookout, eyes wide open for that special one.

Mitch drummed his fingers on the steering wheel to the catchy beat of a song but also with growing impatience. He realised tonight's plan could all go belly up but Hart was growing mentally stronger and more confident again now and had someone in his life to cherish and support him, to give him purpose.

He was getting comfortably acquainted with the feeling himself. A powerful baffling draw toward that other person beyond explanation or reasoning. His Dad had probably brought Darcy back to the homestead by now, he thought idly.

Mitch was about to get out of his ute and go investigate in the hospital to see if there was any sign of Hart and Rose yet when he spied movement at the rear door nearby.

Hart emerged first, scanning the night in every direction before reaching behind him, hand in hand, cautiously drawing Rose forward and making a beeline for Mitch's ute. The second they appeared, he already had the engine running.

Hart kissed Rose, she slid in beside Mitch who gave his brother a thumbs up before they left the hospital and headed west from town. He kept an eye on his rear view mirror but the absence of any headlights suggested they probably weren't being followed.

Rose sat in silence. 'He'll be fine,' Mitch said.

She nodded but, unsmiling, just stared ahead.

'Be about an hour. Try and sleep.'

She shook her head so Mitch let her settle after the evening's upheaval.

As the familiar lights of *Matilda Downs* homestead gradually came into view, Mitch said unnecessarily, 'We're home,' as they pulled up out front to see Elise and Darcy sharing a seat on a step together.

Mitch warmed at the casual chummy sight. The women seemed to have formed a bond the night of Hart's attack on Darcy when Elise had come to the rescue. He shook his head against the regrettable memory.

'The blonde is my sister Elise.'

'Naturally,' Rose finally spoke, a hint of humour in her voice.

'The brunette is Darcy Manning, the lead palaeontologist on our dig. I'm hoping she wants to become a part of the Beaumont family one day.'

'She's stunning. Good luck,' Rose said softly.

The girls rose on the step and came down to greet them. Elise bounced straight up to Rose, introduced herself, took her bag and arm, and led her indoors.

Darcy and Mitch lingered in the dark, standing staring at each other, eyes locked for a long while.

'Come and kiss me, cowboy,' she whispered.

Eyeing off those long legs and that silky dark hair, it had been his intention anyway so he obliged.

When their mutual passion was satisfied, at least for now, Darcy said, 'It's starting.'

'Yep. All happening.' He kissed her again, grabbed her hand and they went indoors too.

Rose fitted into the Beaumont family like she had always belonged. With quiet ease and her natural simple English charm backed by a will of steel, she was swiftly accepted by everyone.

With her reserved assurance, she and bubbly Elise formed a complementary pair, Nina fussed as future grandmothers were entitled to do and Ed just looked on, smiling indulgently, especially at his wife.

Mitch watched Darcy as always comfortably a part of the evening. She constantly eyed Rose with intense compassion, helped Nina serve each course but generally sat back for tonight was Rose's stage, being introduced as an unexpected addition to the family.

And it *was* family, Mitch recognised. Rose was Hart's partner and Mitch had plans for Darcy along similar lines. He knew the catch of his life when he saw it and he didn't plan on letting her get away.

Behind the evening's chatter and warmth and laughter, he was sure Hart's welfare was in the back of everyone's mind. He had put himself out there to help clean up this fossil smuggling mess where he had been on the wrong team. As events had turned out, the family now sheltered under their united wings this cute new English person and her unborn child for whom Hart had clearly fallen in a big way.

By the time a pot of tea took pride of place in the centre of the kitchen dining table along with a plate of Nina's homemade oat biscuits and fruit cake, the conversation mellowed. Into a brief moment of silence Rose confidently took the opportunity to address the issue Mitch was sure lingered unspoken on everyone's mind.

'My appearance must be a shock to you all.'

'Unexpected,' Nina readily agreed, 'but I can assure you an extremely pleasant one. I'm personally so grateful you happened into Hart's life. Just in time it seems.'

'I've travelled loads in recent years and had any number of amazing coincidences in meeting people.'

'Well Nina and I are pleased you ended up around Winton and *Matilda Downs* and bumped into our son,' Ed said. 'Where are you from in England, my dear?' he asked quietly.

'Plymouth growing up. My father was in the Royal Marines so our family was stationed there. They don't move around like other regiments so our life was quite stable actually. But he did serve in deployments to Afghanistan and Iraq.'

'We hear about these wars on television,'

Nina said, 'but you've experienced them firsthand having your father away overseas among the action. How did your family cope?'

'My mother had her own career. She's a nurse in a local large teaching hospital. Military staff train and work there too. And all of us kids were at school while Dad was missing so I guess we kept busy enough really and tried not to think about it. Mum had regular phone and email contact when they weren't away from their base.'

'Is your father still in the services?' Elise asked.

'No.'

Mitch noticed Rose clench her hands tighter around her mug of tea.

'He resigned actually. Something really awful must have happened overseas that he never spoke about because we could see he wasn't the same man back at home. He had counselling sessions but they didn't seem to help.' Rose looked down at her hands and frowned.

'Sorry Rose,' Elise apologised. 'If you don't want to talk about it-'

'No really.' She paused. 'Within two years he...committed suicide.'

A collective gasp of horror and compassion issued around the room from everyone followed by murmurs of sympathy and regret.

Seated beside Rose, Elise reached out a hand to her shoulder. 'Oh hell, Rose, I'm so sorry I asked.'

Visibly shaken and moved by memories, Rose shook her head and pulled a tight grin. 'It's all right. I'm asked sometimes and you have to face it. I don't believe it's something you ever really recover from. At least I haven't yet and it's been five years. I'm the youngest of four so I was still at secondary school when it happened.

'But as soon as I left, I studied psychology at university then I headed out into the world backpacking and travelling to grow my life experience. Sometimes it's hard to tell but I decided never to ignore or turn my back on anyone who showed signs they could potentially be a tormented soul.'

Rose brightened as she continued, the family fascinated in concentration listening to her story. 'Hartley's sadness stood out like the jump up does out here on the plains. He was drinking heavily, appeared to be a loner, not many friends. Occasionally he would strike a conversation or meet a mate but underneath I strongly sensed there was a problem. Trouble is, it's often difficult to start a conversation about it.

'Hartley and I were just friends to start with really, over the bar in the pub, you know? But there was a mutual spark of interest there so I took a leap of faith and went out with him. Dinner at another pub in town on my night off, then he drove me out to the jump up. Well,' she sighed, 'it was a full moon and even in the dark the sight of that vast country was awesome. He had backed up that great big black beast of a truck of his, dropped the tailgate and, honestly, we literally sat talking for hours. It was a quick attraction but it took longer for him to confide. Once I had his trust, it was like flood gates opened.'

Rose glanced between Nina and Ed. 'I would just like to reassure you Mr. and Mrs. Beaumont that I have a solid relationship with Hartley and I have genuinely fallen in love with him.'

More than one pair of eyes glistened with tears around the table. Mitch instinctively searched for Darcy's hand beside him and squeezed it. She turned to him with such love in her eyes it was impossible to resist her mouth in a tender kiss. Despite other emotions swirling around the table, everyone caught the open gesture and not particularly with surprise.

Mitch had noted Rose always referred to his brother by his full name of Hartley. Speaking of him in only a positive way, this petite partner apparently proving to be his salvation.

'Bloody hell, Rose, what a story,' Elise sniffed, rising to grab a box of tissues and setting it on the table for everyone's use, effectively easing the moment with humour. 'But I wish you weren't pregnant so we could have a drink to you and Hart. And the memory of your father,' she added.

Rose stood when Nina approached her

around the table and they hugged. 'It's obvious your love for Hart is returned. We couldn't be happier for you both.'

'If you don't mind, Mrs. Beaumont-'

'Nina.'

'Nina,' she repeated, smiling. 'I might go to bed. I probably shan't sleep but could you please wake me if Hartley calls?' She wrung her hands together across her rounded stomach. 'That Stirling chap is a nasty piece of work. He's only using Hartley because he can access this station for the fossil, and he only wants the other old man Bernie for the airfield on his property. Not sure either of them will see any money. Didn't like him the moment we met when he and Hartley struck a deal. I begged him to walk away but he was convinced this was our opportunity.'

'Did Hart tell you about *our* offer, Rose?' Ed asked with an approving nod from Nina.

'Yes. It's amazing.' She hesitated, staggered, and pressed a hand to cover her trembling lips, her emotions finally emerging. 'You can't imagine what this will mean for him.'

'It's for both of you Rose, and I think we do,' Nina chuckled. 'You're starting a life together. We hope it helps.'

'It will do much more than that.' She turned to Mitch. 'Thank you for bringing me out here tonight,' then nodded to everyone else in general. 'You're an awesome family. When all this is over, Hartley and I plan to visit my mother and siblings in England. Don't worry,' she quickly explained, 'we'll be back for the baby's birth. After that Hartley wants to pursue his dream of a country music career. Possibly get a manager. I think he's way good enough.'

'He's played for you?' Nina asked.

Rose nodded. 'He wants to play at festivals, tour the country, that sort of thing.'

After Rose said goodnight and retired, the awestruck Beaumont family, digesting her confidences and news, realised they had acquired a determined new asset in their family and were stunned yet delighted that Hart had already looked to his future.

Sitting around the lounge, they all decided to wait a while longer in case Hart contacted them with any updates. Nina made more tea but with Rose absent, the consideration of not serving alcohol in her presence was set aside. Ed poured himself and Mitch a brandy on ice while the women opened a bottle of wine.

'Hope it's not presumptuous,' Nina raised her glass, 'but I would like to make a toast to the successful outcome to everything that's happening in our family at the moment. It's certainly keeping Ed and I on our toes.'

'Especially to Hart,' Mitch proposed solemnly. 'I hope he convinces Stirling, gets the information Darcy needs and stays safe.'

Waiting for developments and sweating on

Hart's safety stretched everyone's patience. Small talk fizzled, even lively Elise grew thoughtful, but after an hour and a number of refills all round, Ed frowned.

'Someone's coming.'

Even as they heard its throaty note, a strained Rose appeared in the doorway and said with a shrug of resignation, 'I couldn't sleep. Heard his truck.' She raced down the hallway to meet him.

Being tactful, the family stayed indoors giving the couple time together. Meanwhile Nina gathered up their glasses and removed them to the kitchen while Ed stoppered the brandy decanter and returned it to the sideboard.

After a moment a rumpled Hart, running a hand across his weary face, stepped into the lounge, Rose quietly beside him.

Ed turned at their entrance. 'Glad you're safe, son. Take a seat. What's happening?'

Hart nodded to Mitch and murmured, 'Thanks for bringing out Rose.'

'You're exhausted,' Nina said. 'Anything to eat or drink?'

He shook his head and glanced toward Darcy. 'Stirling's meeting was about getting out to your dig site tonight. Told him you have night patrols and it would look suspicious if I'm prowling around in my truck. I can hardly creep up anywhere in it so I offered to go out early in the morning. He got stroppy. Said he gave the orders.' Hart shrugged. 'He didn't like it.

Seemed set on finding out about that big fossil.'

Beside him, Mitch felt Darcy stiffen and she edged forward on her seat. 'Stirling won't go out and try taking it tonight, will he?' she sounded almost breathless with fear.

Hart scowled and held up a hand. 'Relax. I don't believe so. He won't move without confirmation but he wants it for sure once it's free from the ground.'

Darcy nodded and pressed a hand to her chest. 'It is. Oh my God it *was* his target all along. The sneaky bastard. I've been way too blasé and put all the teams lives in danger.'

'Stirling said it would be the icing on his treasure cake. Was sneering when he said it,' Hart told them. 'He's gonna add it to the collection already out in the cave.'

Darcy pounced. 'He already has stuff?'

Hart nodded. 'His operation have a lease on a fossil site further north the other side of the jump up and he's been mining for specimens.'

Darcy scoffed with exasperation. 'Very smart. It's a private dig so they can take what they like with no protections in place.' She turned to Mitch. 'Surely we have enough intel to go to the police now.'

'If they wait until he actually moves it,' Hart suggested evenly, 'probably tomorrow night, they can track him all the way to his buyer. That way you don't just get Stirling you get the whole ring. The operation he's part of is big. From the way he brags it's, like, international.'

'As it happens, we're moving the fossil in the morning,' Darcy informed him.

'Damn,' Hart said darkly, his mouth twitching into the hint of a grin, 'he's gonna be furious when he hears that but he better not take it out on me.'

'No heroics,' Mitch said with brotherly concern. 'Leave the details to the authorities. We need definite information first.'

'If you don't tell him till after we have the move underway,' Darcy offered, 'it will be too late. There will be people everywhere, a police escort and no chance of theft.'

'Nothing more we can do tonight but looks like action stations for everyone tomorrow,' Mitch said, standing. 'I'll take Darcy back out to the camp.'

'Hart,' Nina said, 'I've changed all the linen in your cottage. Cleaned it up a bit. If you and Rose-'

'Thanks,' he muttered awkwardly. 'I'm not letting her out of my sight. I'll bring her back to the homestead in the morning, contact Stirling again and get word to you when I can.'

'I'll just go get my bag,' Rose slipped away.

As Hartley headed outside, Darcy whispered to Mitch, 'Won't be long,' and followed his brother.

Chapter 14

On the shadowed veranda, only dimly lit from indoors, Hartley turned at the sound of footsteps, probably expecting Rose, so his face clouded like someone hunted when it wasn't the mother of his child.

Darcy was surprised by his alarm at the sight of her. Making the rash decision in the lounge room to speak to him as Hart left, she hadn't really chosen any words to say so her persistent caution kept her feeling distant and awkward.

'Hartley? Um-'

'I know it's not enough but I'm really sorry,' he blurted out.

Darcy didn't accept his apology but she nodded. 'And the drink was doing a lot of the talking.' The air swirled thick with tension between them. 'Still doesn't excuse what you did.'

'Nope.' Silence for a moment. 'Hope it don't

get uncomfortable me being around.'

Darcy shrugged. 'Shouldn't do.'

She wanted to reach out, ease his anxiety, but she couldn't. Not yet. Maybe in time. She was only on *Matilda Downs* for a few more days anyway.

'Rose and I will be away on the road a lot.'

She had no idea why that should affect her and frowned in confusion. 'Yes. Rose mentioned your plans. I hope it works out for you. The dig ends in a few days and I'll be leaving too,' she pointed out.

Hart gave a short laugh without smiling. 'You're gonna be in Mitch's life as much as Rose is in mine.'

Darcy's heart skipped a beat at his perception. 'I am?' She sank her hands into her jeans pockets. 'I guess we'll see.'

'I've been a fool about a ton of things in my life but not that. The way you look at each other-' He gazed out from the veranda across the mysterious unseen star-filled night. 'Mitch is right for you. Rose is helping me work on improving.' His voice lowered a notch. 'Maybe I'll be worthy of her one day.'

Darcy felt surprised to be impressed by what seemed to be his genuine humility. Her stern heart softened a little toward him. 'It's up to you now to make Rose and your child proud.'

'Maybe if you ever trust me again, we can be friends.'

'Maybe. Let's run up a white flag but take it slow, huh?' She fixed him with a steady challenging stare. Hart seemed to be on a better path in his life now but he had a long way to travel before he earned her respect again.

'Appreciate it.'

Floundering for conversation and really having nothing more to say to each other, they left it at that, in the realm of one day and possibilities.

'Good luck with Stirling,' Darcy murmured, walking back inside as Rose reappeared.

When Mitch pulled up in the ute by Darcy's waterhole camp, she sighed. 'Going to be a long night.'

'Want me to stick around?'

She shook her head. 'Ask me that question another time okay? Promise it will be different,' she chuckled, leaning closer across the floor gear shift, running her hand inside his shirt, feeling his heartbeat and body warmth, begging to be kissed.

When he obliged, its heat and promise calmed her. Keyed up over the importance of tomorrow and its pressures for everyone, she allowed the feeling of their mouths dancing together and his big old arms around her to soothe her soul and get her through the next twenty four hours.

Later, watching Mitch's red tail lights grow smaller, filling her with a deep sense of loss, her thoughts were pulled to Stirling. After five years, how close they were to catching him. How Mitch's entire family were now all involved by fate or design in what had previously been her own personal mission. Now thrown open through their unity to the possibility of the best outcome ever.

Her gaze narrowed as she gritted her teeth. The bastard would not get away this time.

Darcy closed her eyes, silently prayed for success, Hart's safety despite their private discord that would take time to heal, and tossed in a little wistful plea of romantic yearning for good measure.

Despite doubling the night patrol, Darcy couldn't sleep and prowled the main camp and dig site, the half-moon gleaming on *Mitch's* plaster shell.

As light on the horizon slowly stole the dark and another golden outback sun rose into a clear blue sky, Darcy had a quick word to Murray on the last watch and strode across to her waterhole camp. She freshened up and changed into jeans and one of her last remaining clean slogan tee shirts for what promised to be a busy and exciting, if bittersweet, day.

Needing to take leave of *Mitch*, entrusting him into other professional hands where work would begin in the preparation laboratory on the process of his exposure and transformation. Museum workers would use a cutting saw to open the field jacket that Darcy and her team had created. It would then be carefully pried open and painstaking progress continue until his actual bone was revealed. Probably when the museum closed over the hot summer.

Darcy looked forward to eventually seeing its reincarnation. She might even volunteer to help and share in witnessing the evolution. Meant she would be closer to Mitch. She didn't need him to tell her that was what he wanted, too. He had already conveyed those sentiments with words and some mighty thorough kissing. Not to mention the countless steady loving gazes he had bestowed on her from the depths of those Beaumont blue eyes.

While the dig team fired up for yet another day, fuelled by Dawnie's breakfast and the excitement of *Mitch's* imminent removal as Darcy supervised it all, it never left the back of her mind that Hart would have told Stirling the bad news by now, that her big guy was beyond his reach. Better still she would have loved to be there and watch his reaction.

Only once their precious fossil treasures were fully safe would she relax. And there was the importance of learning the Professor's moves and timing so Hart could feed it back to them. Then when he contacted them again, the next phase would begin. Depending on what he could learn and if he had a chance to pass on that information, Darcy hoped it was enough facts and evidence to approach the local police.

But for now at the dig site all hands shared in the sometimes heavy, always awkward tasks of guiding and loading the covered fossil pieces onto the museum truck.

For *Mitch*, it took straps attached to the front of the digger teeth and wrapped around him before he could be carefully lifted and settled into place, then secured down for the journey into town. The remaining pallets of fossils were stacked ready to be the next loads, all under close guard.

Although Darcy gave instructions, the museum staff who had escorted the truck had done this before too, relieving her stress of being the sole responsible palaeontologist as she had for the duration of the dig so far.

As the truck slowly drove away, Darcy watched its departure with wonder, diverted when she became aware of Helen at her side.

Darcy folded her arms. 'Do you realise the last time that long necked herbivore plucked branches from a conifer for a snack 95 million years ago this land was a lush forest not a dusty sheep property? And man didn't exist.'

'Good to know,' Helen murmured, the humour in her tone unmistakeable. 'Going to be sad leaving. Gonna need Kleenex but I'm putting my name down for another dig for sure.'

'Bless you. Even despite skinned knuckles and broken fingernails?'

Helen laughed. 'It *has* been hard work but we've all had such fun, made friends and joined in a new experience that has broadened our horizons.'

They fell silent standing together watching the truck finally disappear along the track past the homestead that led back to the main road and into town.

Darcy's head space was on the dig and all that it had been. Her time and the location out here on *Matilda* station. And the biggest find of all? The fossil hunter himself. Who knew that the station owner's son whom Darcy had wrongly assumed was a boy, would turn out to be one sexy outback man?

'Well we have work to do,' Helen sighed and planted her hands on her generous hips. 'Come on, boss. Let's get to it.'

Darcy smiled and followed then spent the following minutes that turned into hours trying to work, totally distracted, waiting for any sign or news from Mitch that might have been passed along from his brother.

When he eventually arrived, she bounded up out of the dig pit area and across to the ute even before he pulled up in a haze of dust.

Mitch climbed from his vehicle leaving the door open and the motor running. 'Hart's been in touch. The job's on. Apparently Stirling was volcanic about my namesake being moved. So now Hart and everyone else on his payroll have been told to head for the jump up cave to load up and get it to Bernie's airfield on *Mulga Plains* so it can be moved offshore.'

'Good.' Darcy's heart pumped with adrenalin. 'What now?'

'I've phoned Winton police and given them the gist and heads up with what's been happening. They're on their way out to the homestead now for a chat. I told them what Hart said, and Glenn agreed, about tracking and not arresting them. But they're onto it. They already have the Border Force involved but they want to interview us at the house. Can you get away?'

Darcy scoffed. 'Can I what! Not missing any of this.' She spread out the fingers of her hand. 'Give me five. I'll be right back.'

She sprinted down into the dig pit and had a quick word to the museum palaeontologists helping now. They were already informed and warned of brewing events. Knowing the importance to their scientific field of what was officially about to go down, they willingly assumed supervising the wind up and tidying of the site.

This freed up Darcy both physically and emotionally to be around and involved for news of developments and the final sting. Her greatest dread was that somehow Stirling would slip the net again. She would die before she let that happen. Even if she had to steal a boat to get out into the ocean and follow him herself.

But of course that wouldn't happen. She knew her passionate thoughts were dramatic but – whatever it took. Operations like this needed to be stopped. Not all fossil smugglers could be caught but surely the police could use Stirling and the organisation he worked for as an example.

As Darcy and Mitch jumped back into the ute, she said, 'Mind if we load my motorbike into the back on the way past?'

'Sure.' Mitch eyed her with amusement.

'Might need to feel the wind in my hair in the coming days. Ease the tension.'

'No need to explain,' he said warmly, reaching out to clasp her hand. 'This is a big deal. I get it. Trust me, I want this for you as much as you want it yourself.'

At the homestead the local police had already arrived, a chequered blue and white patrol car parked out in front. Once inside, Mitch seemed to know them all, greeted them like old friends or mates, and shook hands before introducing Darcy.

With Nina the ultimate hostess yet again handing around cold and hot drinks, the kitchen table was fully occupied with the officers and family.

The younger Tom and older Ross turned out to be great outback guys. Because of the nature of its terrain and location in this mid-west dinosaur country region, both men had been involved with fossil smuggling before. But, by their own admission, nothing like the potential vast extent of this syndicate.

Darcy caught their buzz of interest and was impressed by their brisk efficiency. For them it was clearly all about business, doing their job well and catching their men. She had no doubts that her once personal mission had been rightly transferred into more capable hands.

Mitch coated the truth a little and made it plain that Hartley had unwillingly been blackmailed into cooperating with Stirling but was on the family's side and responsible for delivering the latest information.

Tom led the questioning. 'When you return to Brisbane, we'll need to see all those diaries of yours as background to building our case,' he told Darcy.

Mitch told them about his own investigations with their family lawyer, Glenn Whyte, and how he was convinced vital evidence had been deliberately concealed from Stirling's court hearing years before.

Ed, Nina, Elise and Rose all stayed silent and listening throughout.

When the interrogations concluded, an edgy Darcy said, 'I hate to ask but, ball park figure, how long might this take?'

'Since it sounds like they're taking the goods offshore, we're probably talking at least a number of days. The ABF team is already on the ground and alert in place everywhere else to cover every stage of tracking the smugglers' moves. If they hit the ocean, which seems likely, then it becomes a maritime operation with surface and air vessels. They'll head out with patrol boats and specialist vessels. Don't worry, when they have their target on radar and in sight, they'll pick their moment to launch a tender for fast interception and boarding.'

With assurances of regular updates, the officers left.

Feeling lost, Darcy said, 'What can we do?'

'Nothing,' Mitch replied. 'We wait.'

'Damn. That's going to be hard.'

She was torn between a spin on her beloved motorbike or practising patience, a virtue never in short supply on a dig site but not in this tense situation.

With Hartley so deeply involved undercover in the smuggling action, Rose declined Nina's offer to stay in the house but instead wandered across to the cottage supposedly to rest. But while no one was fooled that she would enjoy a moment's peace, clearly she needed space and time alone.

Elise had momentarily disappeared and now peeked her head around the kitchen doorway. She indicated her camera bags slung over her shoulder. 'Catch you all later. Be at the waterhole.'

Once outside she was heard whistling to her

dogs and sped off in her vehicle for more photo time on her university portfolio project.

With shearing starting in the coming weeks, Ed diverted attention and made the brilliant suggestion that he and Mitch head out to start mustering the flocks. Without waiting to be asked along, Darcy grabbed the opportunity to join them.

While Ed chose his ute, unchained and whistled to his collie sheep dog that leapt into the cab beside him, Mitch jumped on a quad bike with another dog perched on the rear carry rack behind him. Darcy fired up her two wheeler, slapped on her favourite big straw hat and followed them in convoy away from the homestead.

As she rode, Darcy realised she'd had no time to get out and appreciate this country. Despite the rugged conditions, sheep thrived here on the grassland spinifex plains dotted with the low spreading mulga trees. The winding courses of occasional seasonal waterways were identified by coolabah and river gums, strikingly tall against a land of otherwise stunted vegetation.

As they reached the furthest paddocks and the first flocks came into view, the trio and dogs set to work.

Darcy had helped muster cattle on vast Territory stations so she figured sheep couldn't be too different. At their approach, the flock banded together for protection but, apart from an occasional renegade escapee or straggler that the dogs swiftly brought into line by expertly circling the flock and keeping it under control, they behaved themselves.

Darcy was content just to putter along on her bike behind being a part of it all, eating their dust, revelling in slowly helping mile by mile to guide the flock closer into a home paddock. Each group would be brought in on a regular schedule to avoid overcrowding. After shearing, Darcy guessed the animals would be spray dipped against pests then returned to their pastures to be pretty much undisturbed for another year.

During the morning she had spotted more than one red kangaroo grazing, with the early wildflowers of oncoming spring already popping their heads through the grass, creating a beautiful display.

When they returned to the house for a late lunch, Nina had hamburgers grilling on the barbeque and Elise was helping fill buns with salad. Rose quietly reappeared and joined them.

'You okay?' Darcy heard Elise ask her quietly.

Rose nodded and took up a seat among them. With everyone cleaned up, they all sat outside in camp chairs overlooking the mown grass of the rear garden, the dogs happily resting at their feet.

Darcy's heart filled with contentment at the warm genial company around her and the outback tranquillity. In any such setting as this, she always felt like she had come home.

As they ate and shared murmured *safe* conversation, and following such an awesome morning out mustering, it was almost possible to forget the troubling events taking place elsewhere so acutely affecting every member of the family in one way or another.

But a police car cruising up to the homestead mid-afternoon soon shattered the family's few hours of outward serenity.

News.

Darcy was sure every heart, including her own, sent out silent prayers and, with a collective holding of breath, prepared for Tom's latest message.

Chapter 15

With the family outwardly comfortable and gathered once again in the homestead lounge room, Rose particularly pale with apprehension, Tom got right down to it.

'The smugglers have made their move. Spent most of the day so far transferring their haul from the cave to a truck and out to *Mulga Plains* airstrip. Decent medium range Cessna Caravan they're using,' he remarked. 'Means plenty of room for cargo *and* passengers. Should only take them two hours if their destination is Darwin. ABF's onto it and tracking.'

He hesitated. Darcy flashed Mitch a glance. She wondered if any of the others had picked up on Tom's reference to passengers. She held her breath as he proceeded to explain but for Rose's sake crossed her fingers anyway.

'Hartley and Bernie helped all day. At the

airstrip, once the goods were loaded, *everyone* boarded the plane.'

Tom waited for the implications of his words to sink in. It didn't take long. Ed and Nina shared a look of deep concern.

'Including Hartley?' Rose breathed, barely above a whisper, her eyes appealing to him to tell her otherwise.

But he nodded. 'Yes, Ma'am. Afraid so.' Tom glanced among them all. 'You need to know they didn't look willing. Stirling produced a gun.'

Rose wrenched back a sob and placed a hand on her stomach. Elise shuffled closer on the sofa and put a comforting arm around her shoulder.

'Pilot and another man backed Stirling up with muscle and they've just taken off. The men are obviously being kept as insurance so we add deprivation of liberty to the growing list of charges. I can assure you Ma'am,' he addressed Rose alone in lowered tones, 'they're on our radar every minute and they'll be safe while they're flying. We'll get them out as soon as we can after they rendezvous and land.'

No one dared ask how. Whatever method they used and judging by the distraught looks on the faces around the table, everyone just hoped their rescue worked.

'I know it's hard,' Tom said with quiet regret, 'but try and stay positive. I can assure you all this is a carefully planned operation. Next news might be later tonight after they land in the

Territory. We believe they'll try and move the stuff on fast. Border Force has one team in Cullen Bay keeping an eye on Stirling's yacht just in case but we have our doubts they'll use it. Location's too exposed, lit up at night. Be impossible to get past the security gates and avoid the patrols and video surveillance covering the marina.

'This haul is a big one. It will take longer and be more obvious to transfer so they'll be seeking some place isolated and private. The smugglers look like they're getting greedy or cocky or both. When they finished loading out at Bernie's airfield, that Cessna was weighed right down to its limit.'

He donned his police cap and tipped its visor as he left. 'Be in touch.'

Everyone murmured their thanks. After Tom's visit no one felt like eating dinner but Nina made soup and Rose produced fluffy scones.

'Nina's recipe,' she managed a weak smile, still an air of expectant motherly glow beneath her pallor of anxiety.

Darcy decided to take a break and head back on her motor bike to the dig camp. It might be one of the last times she had a chance to see and thank the team all together before they disbanded and went their separate ways.

Mitch followed her out. 'You coming back tonight?'

She nodded. 'Like to be around when there's news.' She pushed back her hair and tipped her gaze to the inky star-riddled night sky. Normally keeping her emotions under control, Darcy felt the need to share. 'I just want this to be over. For Hart to be safe and Stirling caught. Hold me?' she appealed.

Without a word he drew her tight against him and just held her. She wrapped her arms around his muscled chest and rested her head into his neck. They just stood together, breathing in each other's scent, feeling mutual pounding heartbeats and, before too long, not resisting a deep and desperate kiss.

As Darcy legged it over her bike a while later, Mitch lingered and murmured, 'Promise you that real soon we won't have to leave each other.'

He ran his hands up and down her waist, nudging the rise of her breasts and kissed her again, long and hungry and slow. Holy cow, Darcy thought, when they finally got together she would explode. Her heart curled with desire and her whole body throbbed with need.

'Look forward to it,' she whispered, knowing that right this moment she would prefer this man between her thighs instead of a motor bike seat.

It took all her self-control not to haul him off into the dark but she fired up her bike and powered away in the direction of the waterhole and dig camp.

It took a while for her libido to slow down but it was a distraction from everything else going on at the moment to reconnect with the team sitting around the main campfire, laughing, telling stories, with the two new museum scientists, Julie and Bill, joining in.

It made for a great night with a rowdy bunch of people. Wine bottles were opened and beer rings snapped on cans. Mobile numbers and email addresses were swapped and potential lifelong friends made.

Darcy updated everyone on the smuggling operation underway. Knowing that's where her loyalty lay right now, soon after she rose from her camp chair and stretched, willingly submitted to endless hugs and well wishes and took her leave. She had been careful to only accept one beer for the night and checked her own tent and camp was secure before returning to the homestead. Its lights spilled out onto the veranda where Mitch sat on the step, waiting.

'Any news?' she called out as she dismounted, knowing he would have contacted her but asking anyway.

'Nope.'

'How's everyone?' She joined him on the step and he wrapped an arm around her shoulder, snuggling close.

'Rose is holding up but faking. The folks are quiet which means they're worried sick. So

Dad's pretending to read a newspaper and watch television while Mum's baking up a storm in the kitchen using the excuse of filling the freezer ready for shearing. Elise is on her laptop in the office editing photos.'

Darcy released a long sigh. 'Somehow saving a fossil suddenly doesn't seem as important as saving two human lives.'

'Tom told us to have faith so let's stay strong.'

'Okay. Let's go see what Nina has to eat.'

Somewhere around midnight the homestead landline rang in the office. Everyone looked at Mitch who disappeared to answer it. Darcy idly sauntered to the door slightly ajar and pushed it wider to listen. Mitch was pacing, staring at the floor and listening, pretty much a one-sided conversation. At one point his gaze rose to meet hers and he gave the slightest frown and shake of his head.

Damn. Not looking good.

When Mitch hung up, he stood with his hand on his hips staring at her. Please God, not bad news. Not that. Not Hartley. She wrung her hands together. Rose was proving a strong little thing but her composure was being tested and crumbling. Ed and Nina were stretched to their emotional limits. Elise, more sensibly grounded, remained positive, perhaps for the sake of her parents and Rose. And somehow Mitch was outwardly holding it together, an anchor for them all.

'They're alive but still being held,' he murmured.

Holding hands, they moved into the living room to deliver the disheartening news. A little good news wouldn't have hurt. They could all do with a boost.

'What happened?' Rose asked almost angrily after Mitch told them. 'Why didn't they get Hartley and Bernie out?'

'I gather an opportunity didn't arise. Once the plane landed south of Darwin on a remote property there were men everywhere. The unloading and transfer of the fossils was slick and straight onto a big beast of a chopper. Stirling stayed behind but Hart and Bernie were shuffled aboard.

'The police didn't want to open fire and endanger lives or alert the smugglers they were being watched. Would have jeopardised the whole mission. Tom said our local guys should be safe while in flight. Probably just holding them until the operation is done. The chopper's being tracked heading west across the Territory and Western Australia. After that, it's assumed they'll head out to sea to meet a ship.

'Cruising at 125 knots they might be two hours in the air so they should rendezvous in the early hours. Aerial patrols are already searching for a likely vessel. When the chopper and ship tracking coordinates match, they'll wait till the bird lands and make their move.'

Mitch sent a hopeful glance to Rose. 'That's when they'll be able to free Hart and Bernie.'

'They failed last time,' she challenged.

'Different circumstances,' Mitch said calmly. 'They didn't want to compromise the operation.'

'At the risk of two lives.'

'I'm sure they'll do everything in their power to free them,' Elise intervened with firm conviction but no doubt to also help reassure Rose. This ordeal was tense and tough on everyone.

Darcy frowned. 'What about Stirling? You said he stayed behind.'

'That's the one piece of good news. Police waited until the chopper left and Stirling would have believed he was safe and clear. He jumped in a vehicle and was heading north for Darwin. He was followed and arrested.'

Darcy pressed a hand over her mouth and her eyes brightened with moisture.

'They'll have more than enough evidence to charge him. He was involved up to his neck and in charge of digging up the fossils on their lease land and smuggling it out.'

'It's almost an anti-climax,' she gasped. 'He's really in custody?' She smiled through pooling tears. Mitch nodded. 'And their charges will stick?'

'Damn right. They'll also investigate the Professor's personal finances for any generous deposits that might be tucked away in a tax haven. Just be confirming what they already know.'

Darcy couldn't believe this great outcome but she didn't want to make too much of her personal good news after a five year crusade. Two men's lives were still in danger.

But she couldn't resist muttering, 'I want to be there when he has his day in court. I'm going to sit and stare him down with a smile.'

Exhausted, Ed and Nina finally agreed to at least rest on their bed. Rose and Darcy stretched out on sofas, pulled a blanket over themselves and feigned sleep. Mitch yanked the handle on a recliner and settled in for the wait, too. Elise sprawled out on the floor, about the only one to actually fall asleep. Everyone else just dozed or restlessly turned.

The hours dragged. Drowsily, Darcy was vaguely aware of someone moving about the kitchen next door. She heard the kettle singing and murmured voices. Sounded like Nina and Ed had finally given up on trying to sleep.

The shrill of the telephone after dawn set hearts pounding and bodies sprung to alert. Mitch stumbled from his recliner across the hall and into the office. Within moments he was back, handset on loud speaker, a cheeky grin on his suntanned face and giving a thumbs up.

A barefoot Rose had her hands pushed up into her hair, her body stiff with fear. Still talking and listening, Mitch caught her hand and guided her to sit on a sofa beside him, bringing her closer to the phone and the conversation. At the same time he beckoned to his parents hovering at the French doors into the kitchen.

'You still there Mitch?' Tom was saying on the other end.

'Yep mate. Got you on speaker so everyone can hear. Go for it.'

'ABF boys on aerial patrol spotted and tracked the ship. It linked up with the chopper on a small uninhabited atoll at sea. And you won't believe this - just inside Australian territorial waters. The big bird landed on a small beach and stuff was being transferred already by small boat to the ship when they carried out the sting. Hart and Bernie are safe.'

Nina, Ed and Elise all hugged each other while Mitch smiled down on an equally beaming Rose, her eyes full of happy tears. As they rolled down over her cheeks, she brushed them away, laughing with relief.

Darcy closed her eyes and thanked whatever entity existed out there that had led her to her fossil hunter, Glenn Whyte, and the Beaumonts, who had all played a part and pulled together, in Hart's case risking his life, to achieve this awesome result and news.

'Can you give us a few quick details mate?' Mitch asked Tom.

'Hartley and Bernie, were taken from the chopper and left on the beach. Probably to be stranded there after the ship and plane left. They were already basically abandoned when the Border Force boys arrived and boarded the ship to search it. The smugglers were only worried about saving themselves.

'First checks look like the ship is under a flag of convenience. Registered in one country to avoid taxes and inspections while its owners operate in another. Probably belongs to organised crime and fossil smuggling will be just one of their activities.'

Mitch let out a low whistle.

'We'll get your boy home to you as soon as we can,' Tom assured them all.

'Appreciate it mate,' Mitch said.

'They'll need to be questioned and debriefed first so we'll contact you as soon as we can get them on their way. Give us 24 to 48 hours okay?' Tom appealed. 'They're in safe hands.'

'Sure. Thanks.'

'Oh, by the way, the fossils were all seized and are in our possession, too.'

Darcy breathed a deep sigh of relief that the smugglers' haul would be rightly entrusted and lodged into a museum's collection where they belonged. She gave a silent thumbs up to Mitch whose accidental stumbling on bones had triggered all this in the first place, brought her out here and led to Stirling's arrest.

Tom hung up and Mitch returned the phone to the office. For a while, everyone seemed at a loss, lingering about, feeling aimless, not quite knowing what to do with themselves. And although Hart was not yet home among them again, trying to get their heads around normal life or at least taking up where they all left off before the upheaval of recent days had disordered their lives. Each person changed in some way according to their own circumstances.

It had been a long sleepless night but smiles returned to faces again and Rose's mood in particular had visibly lifted. Ed and Mitch hit the showers while Nina and Rose whipped up a breakfast feast of bacon and eggs and pancakes, the two women working companionably together.

Darcy decided to return to camp to pack up her tent. Mitch reappeared, smiling, fresh from his shower, jeans and tee shirt hugging that powerful body, but when she voiced her intention, he softly challenged her decision.

'At least stay for breakfast.'

In bare feet and tossing her a steamy gaze from those blue eyes, how could she refuse? 'I guess I can.'

Her mind wrestled with the uncertainty of what shape any future between them might take. She longed to be alone with him – really alone, like out-in-the-middle-of-nowhere alone – but told herself to be patient. All good things…

She clung to that smouldering promise Mitch had already given. Their moment would come but it had better be soon. She couldn't hold out much longer for some stunning sex.

Almost done with an excessive breakfast she didn't normally eat, a rumble of vehicles and tooting horns alerted everyone to company passing.

'That'll be the team leaving,' Darcy said grinning.

They all traipsed outside onto the veranda as the cavalcade of duggers trailed past the homestead on their way out. Darcy stood on the front steps waving.

Murray wound down his motorhome window and called out, 'Heading for the coast then south.'

'Safe travels.'

Dawnie and Helen and the other *girls* of a certain age, young of spirit, all madly waved and whistled shamelessly at Mitch standing behind her.

Rather than yelling across the yard, Darcy jogged down the steps and over to the vehicles to inform the local museum palaeontologists and team in general of the great news about the fossil recovery operation.

'Another reason to celebrate,' Helen laughed. 'See you next time,' she called out as they revved up again and began rolling away in convoy.

Chapter 16

Darcy stood for a while watching the dig team procession grow smaller until only their dust clouds remained visible, hovering in the air and finally fading. It always felt like a part of her was left behind after another dig ended.

She crossed her arms and rubbed them. Sensing Mitch close behind she knew she could no longer delay the inevitable so she turned to him.

'It will take me two days to ride back to Brisbane. I should decamp and get moving. If I leave within the hour I should make the national park again for an overnighter.'

'I hope you don't want to go.'

She shook her head. 'Of course not.'

'Good because I don't want you to leave either.'

'But your family needs to regroup, and shearing's looming.' She expressed his thoughts and the reality of his obligation and life on the land that hung unspoken between them.

'The shearing contractors will be arriving any day now. Dad will need all the help he can get. When Hart returns it's unlikely he and Rose will stick around.' He rattled off a whole bunch of reasons.

'And I need time to process everything that's happened these past two weeks. Get my city legs again. And there'll be Stirling's court hearing. Plus I'd love to get back home to Darwin and visit my family. I haven't even had a chance to call them yet. They'll be stoked.'

'So, the second the fleece comes off the last sheep, I'm coming to get you.'

Darcy butted her head into his chest and groaned, his steely arms wrapping around her tight. 'Not sure I can wait that long,' she muttered.

'If we make love now,' he whispered in her ear, 'neither of us is going anywhere. We both have loose ends to tie up, right?'

'Damn,' she cursed. 'Life.'

They broke apart.

'I'll come out to the waterhole in the ute behind you and help pack up, okay?'

Darcy pressed her open hands on his chest and looked up at him. 'Would you mind if I go out alone? A private goodbye will be hell. I'll stop by on my way back. I want to see the rest of your family, too.'

Mitch shrugged. 'Sure but I warn you now, my public goodbye won't leave a single thing to the imagination.'

Not much phased Darcy but the twinkle in Mitch's eyes as he had growled out his declaration had her blushing from head to toe as she finally took her leave and, with a roar of her motor bike, rode away.

At the waterhole Darcy made short work of dismantling her tent and swag, rolling them up tight and small for packing. She took one last look around the dig site, double checking all was restored until another excavation team came out again next winter season.

And sat a moment at the water's edge watching the warming sun of the winter day sparkle on its surface. Birds splashed and squawked and fluttered as they arrived and departed, played and fed. Preening themselves and paddling among the reeds. She closed her eyes to imprint the image on her mind until she returned.

She fired her bike into life again, sat astride and rumbled back to the homestead an hour later.

Self-consciously, she realised the entire Beaumont family waited on the veranda in cane chairs, sitting on the steps, while one particularly gorgeous country boy lounged against a post. As Darcy dismounted, they all came down to meet her.

'No speeches. She'll be back,' Elise quipped, sending them all into laughter, breaking the ice that tended to exist at times like these. 'I'll be returning to Brisbane soon myself for the last term. Can we catch up?'

'Absolutely.'

Nina and Ed hugged her with murmurs of *Don't stay away too long* and *Lovely to meet you, my dear*.

As Rose stood aside, serenely confident again, Darcy said, 'Take care.'

'Hartley will be home tonight,' she beamed.

'Wonderful.'

It felt appropriate that she should be gone before Hart arrived back so the family could reunite in private.

And then there was only one. Darcy's heart almost stalled at the hungry look of possession Mitch tossed her way as he grabbed her hand and they walked to her bike. He didn't waste time. He crushed her against him so she could hardly breathe and his arms slid about her waist.

Hers snaked up around his neck so she could feel and breathe every inch of him as he stole her lips and they kissed as though they needed each other for survival. With desperation and heat. The world around them vanished, lost.

Slow clapping and lusty outback whistles from Elise brought them back to reality. 'Mitchell Beaumont you have no shame. You'll be embarrassing the woman,' his sister called out.

'Loving every moment, Elise,' Darcy chuckled

amid the last of Mitch's hugs and sweet kisses.

From the veranda, she thought she faintly heard Ed say something like, 'Brings back memories, doesn't it, dear?'

To which Nina replied, 'It surely does.'

Before she broke down or changed her mind and stayed, Darcy clipped on her helmet, blew Mitch a kiss, waved to everyone else and left.

For some kilometres, she was in emotional shock and withdrawal from leaving Mitch behind.

She cried with happiness that goddamn Stirling was in custody and would get his due at last, and let the wind blow away her tears. The best therapy was exactly what she had planned. This. Feeling the wind in her face, blowing away the debris in her mind, easing the burden of recent years and helping restore her soul.

But she also burst with hope and burned with desire, already greedy to see the sexy country boy who now owned her heart and who she couldn't wait to see again.

Camping under canvas beneath the stars, her motorbike wheels slowly eating up the bitumen, its powerful engine throbbing beneath her. The endless horizons. She drank it all in until she could escape outback again.

Toward sunset the following day she hit the rush and noise of Brisbane, a marked contrast after the bush quiet of recent weeks. She returned to her rented riverside apartment, unpacked – which didn't take long – and shopped for supplies in her nearest corner store.

And next day returned to work at the museum.

Mitch phoned every night after shearing. She dragged the sound of his sexy deep voice into her body and wrapped it around her like a blanket. She had never known the hours of each day and week to crawl with such frustrating weariness.

So she eased the wait by taking a four-day weekend and flying home to Darwin. The balmy tropical air, so familiar to her since childhood, thawed her last lingering worries as she allowed herself to be spoiled, swam in the pool, pestered Jock in his café, and reminisced with Laura and Dave about Grandpa Joe, knowing how proud he would be of what she had persisted to achieve.

Each night her family gathered on the sprawling back deck at dusk drinking fruity cocktails with umbrellas or ice cold beer, inhaling the aroma of barbecuing meat or sizzling seafood.

Jock took time away from the café when he could and Andy drove in from the cattle station property where he worked to spend time with her, too. The visit doubly appreciated because it was a six hour trip for him into Darwin and six hours back.

Because any man in Darcy's life was a

curiosity, it took her most of the weekend to hint that there might just be someone special in her life. Years ago her family had quickly learned you didn't ask questions about her love life. That she would share details when she was ready. So Darcy left it at that. They knew. Anything more she hugged privately to herself until she had more to tell about her romance, unsure where it was exactly headed.

So it was with contentment that she boarded her Sunday evening flight back to Brisbane.

As it happened Darcy and Mitch discovered from their daily chats that the end of shearing and his arrival in Brisbane coincided with Professor Stirling's court hearing.

At the airport days later, Darcy waited anxiously, fearful the looming court case would somehow diminish or overshadow her happiness at seeing Mitch again. He told her he was driving the three hours into Longreach and taking a late morning direct flight into the city.

As she paced with excitement at the Qantas airport gate, straining for a glimpse of her man for the first time in weeks that had felt like the sluggish passing of agonising years, she saw him. A tall blonde Adonis striding head and shoulders above and among the line of passengers streaming from his flight into the terminal passenger lounge.

He wore light chinos, a black shirt – collar up. Very sexy. And when he caught sight of her, also a knowing private smile. When he reached her, despite people crowding them on all sides, she was swung her off her feet and madly kissed.

Darcy couldn't stem a beaming smile and laughter. In his arms, she was back home and loved.

In Mitch's eyes, Darcy Manning was perfection. And she never failed to surprise and delight. He loved her in any clothes she wore and tonight planned to do exactly that in none at all.

But so far out on *Matilda Downs* he had only seen her in tight jeans and dinosaur tee shirts, her long dark hair up in a ponytail caught in a cap or half hidden under a motorbike helmet or her favourite well-loved straw hat. But holy country honey, if he'd been wearing it today she would have knocked off his old faithful Akubra.

She wore a crazy little floral dress in the colours of ripe peaches, yellow flowers and gum leaves that floated above her knees. His first thought? Boy he was going to enjoy taking that off real slow later. And not where she might imagine. He had plans. But was saving that up as a surprise.

Then his gaze travelled all the way down her long bare tanned legs from the hem of her cute little number to her feet hidden in short etched boots. He'd never seen her legs before but, like everything about Darcy, it was so worth the wait.

Catching his stare and grin on her brown leather Westerns, she said, 'Boots go with anything.'

Mitch smiled indulgently. 'They sure do. In your case, perfectly.'

After their initial burst of kissing he followed it up with linked fingers and more warm pecks on her cheek. Because she was simply irresistible. Just the sweet smell of her and touching her body sent shock waves through his. Thoughts of this gorgeous lady had kept him going all through shearing.

He held out his arm, she took it and they strolled, grinning stupidly at each other, out to the carpark. Although his head was filled with loving, he knew they had business to attend to first.

'What time's the court hearing?' he asked.

Darcy whipped out her mobile and checked it. He'd never seen her wear a watch, showing she wasn't particularly fussed about time. His kind of woman. But then he already knew that.

'An hour. We'll make it.'

'You brought your overnight bag with spare clothes?'

'Yes. You still won't tell me where we're going after the hearing?'

'Nope.'

'Wipe that smug grin off your face, Beaumont,' she said playfully. 'I'll find out.'

She led him to a compact blue SUV and drove

them into the city law courts in George Street. Once inside they found the right courtroom and weren't seated long in the outer public waiting space before it was time for Professor Stirling's case to be heard.

It looked like Darcy wanted to be sure Stirling saw her because she led him to sit in the front row of the public seating area inside.

Darcy watched the Magistrate enter and sit up front facing everyone in the courtroom. Then Stirling was led in from a side door. It pleased her to see the jolt of surprise on his face at the sight of her and she made sure she stared him down, unsmiling, just like she promised herself. Hoping her revulsion spoke for itself.

In his usual designer suit he looked untouchable and squeaky clean but this time hard evidence spoke for itself. Darcy had given Glenn Whyte all of her diaries and notes, Bima's statement and made one herself but would not be called as a witness.

Memories came rushing back of another time and place in another courtroom. She could have allowed herself to be bitter and overwhelmed but instead she drew on a hugely satisfying sense of justice finally being served, straightened her shoulders and silently begged for this criminal to be convicted.

Only then would she feel vindicated in having pursued this thankless tedious journey to prove her original allegations and reclaim her dignity and reputation.

As proceedings began Darcy simply prayed that Stirling not get away this time. He could afford the best lawyers but she hoped they failed. She clasped Mitch's hand tight prepared for a long session but was immediately amazed to hear that Stirling pleaded guilty to all charges. Which apparently meant the Magistrate could deal with the case and pass a sentence. Darcy knew the Professor's surrender must have hurt him something awful which thrilled her to the core.

With her fingers crossed and her whole body stiffening in anticipation, the Magistrate announced that he wished to send a message to others with similar intentions.

Glenn had already warned them that a penalty imposed by a Magistrate was usually lower than in higher courts. So she had prepared herself for Stirling receiving a rap on the knuckles and a fine. If that happened she would be gutted. She mentally rubbed her hands together with delight. That scenario was not looking likely.

Even from a side view, Darcy watched Stirling's mouth pinch into a narrow line and his suntanned face go pale as it was announced his sentence would be a fine of twenty thousand dollars and one year in gaol followed by another year of supervised criminal probation.

Darcy wanted to jump up and scream, *Yes! Take that you bastard.*

Instead she gasped with relief and her stomach did a happy dance. This was so much more than she hoped. Mitch squeezed her hand and before the hearing was adjourned, learned that other investigations into fossil smuggling were now being opened around the country, putting individuals and organisations on notice.

Her only disappointment in the whole proceedings - and they were rather fading into insignificance in the light of the sentence just passed – was that Glenn advised them Stirling could appeal. Darcy hoped he wouldn't be so arrogant as to pursue such a useless waste of time. But if so, that his plea would be dismissed.

She stood, privately gloating as a broken and disgraced Professor left the courtroom under escorted guard.

Chapter 17

As Mitch left the court building hand in hand with Darcy, once out on the street she threw out her arms in front of him and laughed.

'I need to celebrate.'

Flashing her his cheekiest smile, he said, 'Can you wait for half an hour till we're back out at the airport?'

She latched onto his hint fast. 'We're flying somewhere?'

She twirled around which Mitch enjoyed, not only to see the woman of his dreams deliriously happy but also in appreciation of the sexy view as her skirt flared out and revealed even more leg.

'Only for you,' Darcy murmured, catching his roving eye.

Mitch chuckled. 'Okay, back to the airport.'

This time he offered to drive because they weren't going to the main airport. Instead he turned off toward a private terminal.

'Where are we going?' Darcy was onto him immediately, throwing him an intrigued glance.

'Patience, honey,' Mitch said as he pulled up and tossed her car keys to a waiting attendant for valet parking.

He grabbed their bags and she strode after him toward a private charter plane where a pilot and crew waited. On board as the door was locked, they settled into the plush softness of cream leather seats and were offered a selection of drinks by a courteous classy male flight attendant in a crisp white shirt, bow tie and a sharp crease in his trousers even Stirling might have envied.

Clicking her seatbelt, Darcy leaned close and whispered, 'Are we going out to one of the islands on the reef?'

Mitch winced with concern but shook his head. Hell, he hoped she wasn't disappointed. From the corner of his eye, he watched Darcy closely for every emotion and reaction. Had he pegged her correctly? Done the right thing? He wanted tonight to be a special memory because it was the beginning of the rest of their lives to be remembered always.

'Okay,' she murmured, glancing out the window as they took off and the plane immediately banked left. 'We're not heading north along the coast or east out over the ocean.'

She turned and levelled her gaze with his, her flashing brown eyes alive and sparkling. 'We're heading west. Inland. You still won't-?'

Mitch shook his head. 'You'll know when we land.'

'How long?'

'Two hours give or take.'

After one glass of champagne and as they cruised above the clouds into a glorious coral sunset, Darcy reclined her seat and dozed. Mitch suspected in relief and exhaustion. Today and its lead up must have been an emotional drain. She needed a break in isolation and he intended on giving it to her.

From time to time, his gaze travelled over the sleepy woman beside him, long dark bedroom hair tumbling softly about her face and bare shoulders. He throbbed with longing to kiss those full vulnerable lips that didn't need any embellishment, being perfectly luscious as nature intended. She had kicked off her boots leaving her bare legs and feet drawn up and on display.

Mitch couldn't believe this was all his. Admiring the country honey beside him, he hoped he shaped up equally well tonight. Compared to his beautiful Darcy, he hoped his own physique ticked a few of her boxes as well.

She only stirred as the plane engine reduced throttle and they descended to land. She stretched like a sleepy feline and rewarded him with a gentle smile.

'We're landing.'

She straightened her seat and looked out the window into the gathering dusk as the ground rose up to meet them and they touched down with only the slightest bumps.

They alighted and walked away from their plane that looked rather fancy on this rather short remote airstrip. A familiar ute was parked nearby. Darcy stood hands on hips and boots firmly planted in red outback dirt, her brows dipped in thought. None of it would be familiar but she was a smart chick and would soon work it out.

Mitch rattled keys in his pocket and dumped their bags in the back. 'Jump in.'

'We're somewhere on *Matilda Downs*,' she said, climbing in beside him. It wasn't a question but a process of elimination.

'Nope.'

'But the jump ups right over there,' she protested, pointing ahead of them.

'Yep.'

'Somewhere close to *Matilda Downs*.'

'Yep.'

She pulled a wide satisfied smile. 'Your place!'

'Bingo.'

Darcy relaxed, closed her eyes and sighed. 'Wonderful. Anywhere outback suits me just fine.'

Mitch took that to mean she wasn't disappointed after all and grinned to himself.

After five minutes driving on a bush track, they pushed through overhanging coolabahs to an opening concealing a waterhole, rising moonlight sheening its surface, a cottage nestled among the gums at its edges.

Darcy sat forward. 'Does your station have a name?'

'Not yet. Open to suggestions.'

Before the ute had barely stopped, she was out, pulling off her boots and wading into the water. The outback spring was already growing hot and it had been a long day. Darcy did a curved dive like a dolphin spiking into the water then, in a lazy crawl, swam out to the centre. Mitch shook his head. She was a fish.

He unloaded their bags and opened up the cottage. He had spent two days ferrying in supplies, giving it a thorough clean and making it into a cosy love nest.

When his water goddess emerged, pushing back her long saturated hair, water dripped and slid all over her and the thin wet dress sucked and clung to every curve of her amazing body.

Striding straight up to him, she chuckled, 'Eat your heart out country boy.' Then she pressed her soggy self hard up against him.

'You, my beautiful honey, are begging to be loved,' Mitch growled, scooping her up into his arms.

In pure ecstasy, Darcy threw her arms around

her big man's neck then kissed and nibbled her way over every inch of bare skin she could find within reach.

Her loved up gaze drifted over the cottage as they walked through just long enough to register the interior was neat and reasonably modern but decidedly rustic. A couple of plump saggy sofas guarded the open fire place but there was no time to witness more because they were in the bedroom now, king sized she noticed with pleasure, beautifully made up with fresh white linen and a patchwork lightweight fluffy doona. A long paned window looked out onto nothing but private bushland. And he had lit candles?

Mitch let her slide from his arms. 'Need to dry off first?' he murmured.

'I think our heat will do that, don't you?' She raised her arms and stood waiting.

He didn't need asking twice. He caught on real fast and rolled her damp dress up over her head. She hadn't bothered wearing a bra. It was always destined to come off anyway. So that only left white lace knickers.

While Mitch hauled her close for the first of countless hard impatient kisses, she undid his shirt buttons, belt and zipper, desperately pushing it all off his body.

Darcy ran her hands all over the packed and suntanned warm flesh. His jocks bulged so she set him free and wriggled out of her own last flimsy piece of clothing to pool at her feet.

Mitch grabbed her buttocks tight and ground their bodies together while the physical heat burned between them and kissing chemistry blew their minds. They tumbled back onto the bed, Mitch kneeling over her, rubbing himself in the moist excited place that had been waiting for him all her life.

'Get me lost, cowboy,' she breathed, combing her fingers deep into his thick wavy hair.

He smelled so good. Of outdoors and mint and his mouth drew fire from her breasts that he ravished until she shot with a bolt of release all the way south where it was supposed to.

He must have sensed when she was gasping, seeing stars, mindless with sex getting hotter every second. Just as she cried out in spasm he slid deep and full inside her. Dreamily sated, Darcy knew this moment in his arms only confirmed he would be forever in her heart.

As they recovered, he drew her into his arms and, facing each other, kissed her tenderly, both glowing with love. Darcy knew she wanted to be the one that made his days better. Every single one of them.

'If this is a sample, I'm going to love making memories with you,' Mitch whispered against her mouth.

Darcy chuckled and squirmed against him, running her hands in lazy circle caresses all over the body she knew now belonged to her. 'I fell in love with you because of all the little things you don't even know you're doing.'

'I love you so damned much.' He kissed her deeply again, hungrily.

For quite a while they didn't leave the bed. Night had long ago fallen around them as they made love again and dozed, softly flickering candlelight casting dim shadows around the room.

Only hunger for food and not each other drove them to stagger from bed, shower together and drag on tee shirts and shorts before heading outside. The mild and inky dark evening sparkled overhead with stars in the clear outback sky.

Mitch lit an open fire between the cottage and the water, soon spitting sparks, orange flames leaping skyward. He poured them a glass of beer.

'Civilised huh? No can?' she teased.

They clinked glasses while Mitch tossed freshly caught and filleted golden perch into a pan over the coals.

'Fish and beer. This is heaven,' Darcy said.

Within minutes the sizzling juicy white flesh was done and they picked it apart in their fingers straight from the pan.

Over tin mugs of tea later, Darcy asked, 'So, you planning on living out here?'

'Depends.'

She glanced around. 'Looking forward to seeing it properly in daylight. Like what I've seen so far.'

'Best view is from the jump up at sunrise,' he hinted.

Darcy moaned. 'Okay. So long as you don't keep me awake all night.'

'Not sure I can guarantee that.'

But somehow he did. Almost.

While it was still dark, Mitch shook her gently awake. Still only half awake, she followed his lead, dragged on a tee shirt and jeans and climbed into the ute. They sped across the uncleared natural grass plains until they reached the rocky track that ascended the mesa.

At the top, flashing torchlights ahead they walked along a red rocky trail to a lookout. Sitting cross legged on the edge together, they watched the darkness slowly lighten and the day reveal the flat countryside rolling away below in all its ochre wilderness from the escarpment where they were perched.

'Nothing like a beautiful country sunrise,' Darcy sighed with the deepest contentment she had ever known. 'To think all this dramatic dry landscape was created by water. Kind of ironic, huh?'

These days the vast plains of the channel country further west were only wet when its braided watercourses joined up in a flood.

'And your friends the dinosaurs roamed the land.'

'Yeah, unbelievable. Who knew the outback

held such hidden treasures from another time?'

Mitch twined his fingers through hers. 'I've found a treasure of my own.'

'Aww.' Darcy leant her head against his shoulder. 'That's so corny but I love it.'

Mitch nodded to the endless outback view before them. 'All this could be yours, too,' he suggested softly. 'If you want it,' he quickly added.

'It could?'

She hardly dared breathe at what he was hinting and slowly turned to face him, drinking in the sight of her gorgeous lover and boyfriend, unshaven face ruggedly handsome with a shadowed chin. Sandy hair being ruffled by the breeze sweeping up from below.

'If you wanted to live out here, of course.'

'Of course.' Any girl with half a brain knew what was coming so she waited.

'Not aiming to pin you down. Won't be taking you away from your dinosaurs and your career.'

'Can't see that being a problem. I know this bloke who owns a station right smack bang in the middle of dinosaur country.'

'Darcy, honey, I just want to be your man. For life.'

That he should say it so coyly after all the love making they had done last night was simply adorable.

'Well, I'm kind of old fashioned, too.' She scrunched up her nose. 'It's a girl thing. To be sure no other country babe sets her eyes on you, I want the wedding and the ring. Doesn't need to be flashy so long as you're the one sliding it onto my finger.'

'So, you asking me to marry you, then?' he teased, grinning.

'Hell yeah.' Their eyes met and there was no need for words. The deep love shining in their gaze said it all. 'Well, I'm hungry. I need breakfast. Make me smile, cowboy. Take me fishing.'